Close Enemy

by

Sandra Dailey

This is a work of fiction. Names, characters, places, and incidents are either the product of the author's imagination or are used fictitiously, and any resemblance to actual persons living or dead, business establishments, events, or locales, is entirely coincidental.

Close Enemy

COPYRIGHT © 2015 by Sandra Dailey

Cover Art by *Debbie Taylor*

The Wild Rose Press, Inc.
PO Box 708
Adams Basin, NY 14410-0708
Visit us at www.thewildrosepress.com

Publishing History
First Crimson Rose Edition, 2015
Print ISBN 978-1-5092-0382-6
Digital ISBN 978-1-5092-0383-3

Published in the United States of America

"I don't think that's a good idea.
Petrov is just waiting to find you out in the open."

"I can't see my mother because of him. Now you're telling me I can't go to a heavily guarded courthouse? When did you become my keeper?"

"When I got you out of jail and brought you here."

"Whoa, wait a minute, Cal," Connor interrupted. "Maybe we can arrange something."

"Don't try to change my mind, Con. We don't know where Petrov or his thugs are going to be. I don't want to put everyone at risk if he decides to go for her. My focus needs to be on Rosie tomorrow."

"If I'm such a problem, maybe I should find somewhere else to stay!" Leah shouted.

"Don't be ridiculous. If you had anywhere else to go, you'd have already left."

"Ridiculous?" Leah was white hot with fury. "I'll pack our things now. I'd rather live on a bench at the bus station than stay here another minute."

"Leah!"

"Shut up, Caleb, just shut up." Connor stepped between them. "If you let her leave with that baby, I'll hold you responsible for what happens to them."

"Why not?" Caleb scoffed. "After a single night of sex I'm completely responsible for her. She decided to have a baby, without my knowledge, and I'm responsible for her too. She gets thrown in jail, and who has to take care of that? Me, that's who. Now, I'm responsible for her cellmate. Not to mention her booze-guzzling, pill-popping mother who married the ex-con who murdered her sticky-fingered husband.

CLOSE ENEMY is a companion book to previously released *COMMON ENEMY*. Like the twin brothers featured in them, they stand alone, but together they tell a broader story.

~*~

Other Sandra Dailey titles
available from The Wild Rose Press, Inc.:
THE CHIEF'S PROPOSAL
TWICE THE TROUBLE

Dedication

For my daughter, who's given me much joy,
three beautiful granddaughters,
and one amazing great-granddaughter;
Emilee, Cassandra, Jessica, and our new little Sonja.
Remember, there's no shame
in needing a hand up now and then.
Everyone stumbles as they chase their dreams.
I love you, Myriah.

Chapter One

The woman's letter haunted Caleb all night. The smooth, delicate scroll of her handwriting put him in mind of long ago when feather quills were dipped in inkwells. Who used pen and paper to communicate these days?

Everyone used a smart phone for everything from a simple text to bank transactions. But, of course, jails didn't allow smart phones.

They did have landlines for inmates to communicate with their family, friends, and attorneys. He was none of the above, at least not to her. He'd never heard of this woman.

The man he'd spoken to when he called the jail said Caleb's was the only name on Miss Fletcher's visitor list. She'd refused to see anyone since she arrived seven months earlier. Most inmates wanted as many visitors as possible to help fill their lonely hours behind bars.

Why would a complete stranger ask for him by name? The envelope containing her letter had been sent to his law office and forwarded to his home. Block letters across the back of the envelope read PERSONAL, but no information was revealed. It was the tone of the message inside that caused him to drive across town with only half a cup of coffee in his stomach.

Dear Mr. Caleb McCrae,

It's imperative that I speak to you regarding a personal matter. A life depends on your immediate response. Please visit as soon as possible.

Sincerely,

Leannette Fletcher

What kind of name was Leannette? It was one he would have remembered if he'd ever heard it. Even the simple last name was foreign to him.

Minutes after Caleb had turned off Broadway in downtown Tampa he spotted the entrance to the jail. He parked in the half empty lot and walked to the gate taking a mental inventory of the items in his pockets: wallet, keys, pen, and loose change. All would be confiscated during his visit. Experience showed that just about anything could be used as a weapon. It only took twenty minutes to be cleared and another five to be escorted to the visitor's room.

Caleb sat in a plastic chair in front of a glass window with a telephone mounted on each side at his right. The chair across from him was empty. After five more minutes an inmate was led to the door. When she came into view through a large window, his heart skipped a beat. It was her, Leah.

Her dark ringlets had grown to barely brush her shoulders and looked dull. Her face was pale and sad, but he was sure she was the girl who'd written.

She raised her handcuffs to be checked. The orange scrub top was so big on her the shoulder seams fell several inches down her thin upper arms. There was a chain attached to the cuffs that would be hooked to a belt around her waist. Her feet were probably shackled too. Didn't they know she was harmless? Caleb rubbed his temples to ward off a gnawing ache. The man on the phone had said seven months. Almost the entire time he'd looked for her, she'd been right here…serving a jail sentence. How had this happened to such a gentle soul? She couldn't be the woman he'd thought her to be.

When the door opened, she shuffled to the chair across from him. The chains from her wrists and between her feet probably weighed as much as she did. There wasn't a belt at her waist, though. It hung around her hips…under her basketball-sized belly. Caleb's stomach twisted and he felt a little lightheaded. She was, without a doubt, pregnant.

****

It took Leah a moment to wiggle into the seat. She had plenty of room, but the chair legs had been bolted to the floor. She didn't have good use of her hands and her balance was a little off these days. The heavy ankle shackles would doubtlessly cause her legs to swell more than usual. At least she had a few minutes to rest her back. Sharp twinges had plagued her all morning. Having a baby wasn't for sissies, especially when you were in a place where no one cared about the tiny life inside you.

When she finally had a chance to look up she was surprised by the shocked and sickly expression on Caleb's handsome face. Was it the fluorescent lighting or had he actually turned a pale shade of green? His mouth was moving, but it was impossible to hear from her side of the glass. She picked up the telephone receiver on the wall next to her and pointed to his, urging him to do the same.

"Leannette…really?"

"I go by Leah, but they make me use my full name on correspondence." Leah hated her given name. It seemed ridiculously long and elaborate.

"I didn't expect to run into you today," Caleb scoffed. "You never mentioned your last name when we met. It seems there's a lot you didn't tell me about yourself."

"I don't give strangers my name."

"Even when you have sex with them?"

Leah didn't know how to respond. Why did he have to put it like that? Couldn't he just say *sleep with* instead of *have sex with*? It wasn't as though she did such a thing as a habit. She'd never taken a man home from a bar before Caleb and he'd been the last as well. Of course, he didn't know that. She took him home that first night. And then he sneaked out while she slept, without even leaving a note.

Something about Caleb had attracted her like no other man. He hadn't been suggestive or aggressive like most men who came to the Blue Moon Gentleman's Club. He'd been courteous, kind, and friendly. Also, there'd been sadness in his eyes that made her feel he'd seen as much hardship as she had. She'd felt they were kindred spirits. Where was that tenderness now?

To him she was just a trashy cocktail waitress. That's all she must have meant to him the night they were together. Maybe this wasn't such a good idea, but no other choice came to mind.

"How did you get into this mess?" Caleb blurted.

"Are you asking about my situation or my condition?"

"The latter isn't exactly a mystery." Caleb rubbed his temples with his free hand, drawing Leah's attention to his soft, wavy, blond hair. "How did you know I was an attorney? For that matter, how did you know how to contact me? All I got from you was a first name, and not even your real one."

"There was a story in the newspaper shortly after we…met. It was about a man who'd been killed. You were in a picture they printed of the funeral. You were helping carry the coffin. I did an internet search of the names they listed for the pallbearers until I found you. It was just out of curiosity at the time. I wasn't planning to stalk you or anything."

"Do you understand that I don't practice criminal law? I deal with family issues, divorces, custody cases, things like that." Caleb took a deep breath and shook his head. The area between his clear blue eyes drew into a tight knot. "Tell me what happened and I'll see if I can find the right person to help. What are the charges against you?"

"It's too late for that. I was arrested six months ago for possession of stolen goods."

"You're a fence? Do you actually deal in stolen merchandise?"

"Of course not," she groaned. "All I know is, I had just gotten home and gone to bed. It must have been around three in the morning. The cops literally broke down my door. It was terrifying. They had a search warrant." She groaned again. "Maybe I should start from the beginning. You see, a couple had been mugged in their driveway the night before. The man was pistol-whipped by his attacker. A little bit later, someone called in a tip that I had their jewelry and credit cards. The items were found in a box under my sofa. I was assigned a public defender. She tried her best, but the evidence was damning and I couldn't give the name of the assailant. They sentenced me to a year, but I hope to be out after nine months."

"Why didn't you just surrender the guy's name? The cops can protect you if you're afraid of him." Caleb rolled his eyes. "Please don't tell me you took the fall for a boyfriend. It's the oldest and most stupid story in the world."

"Do I look like an idiot? I don't have a boyfriend. I don't know where that stuff came from."

"Well, I don't believe it just grew under your sofa. And, pardon me for stating the obvious, but you must have had a boyfriend at some point." Caleb pointed to her sizable belly. "What happens when Elvis decides to leave the building?"

"When babies are born here, they're placed in foster care, unless a family member claims them. That's why I asked you to come. I need you to figure out how to keep my baby safe. I don't want it lost in the system."

"Don't you have any family?"

"Just my mother," she sighed. "My grandmother and aunt both passed away. I don't know where my cousins live. They both changed their last names when they got married."

"But, your mother is still alive." He looked relieved. "If she's not financially equipped to care for the baby, there are programs that can help. She can bring the baby to see you and keep it safe until you get out."

"No!" Leah looked around to make sure her outburst hadn't alarmed the guard. "I don't want her near my baby. She's not fit to take care of an alley cat."

"Then what about the father? If he doesn't want the baby, perhaps a relative of his would take it in."

"No," she said, more quietly this time. "I don't know if he'd want it or not, but I can't risk a custody battle. What chance would I have in front of a judge? I worked in a strip club. It doesn't matter if I took my clothes off or not. That's probably the only kind of job I'll be able to get when I get out of here. Job opportunities are going to be crap now that I've been convicted of a felony. Besides that, I don't have a lot of confidence in the judicial system any more. After all, look where I'm at. I didn't have anything to do with that robbery."

"If the father cares about you, he should want to take care of you both."

"Well, he doesn't care. Besides that, no one has ever taken care of me. I'm smart enough to know I can't count on anyone but myself."

"Geez, are you this cynical about everything? This is a side of you I've never seen before."

"Caleb, we only spent a few hours together. We don't know each other. I'm not usually so negative, but this is a desperate situation. My baby's welfare is at stake."

"I think you may be selling the father short. I suspect you haven't even told him." Caleb slumped back in his chair. "Give me his name. Let me talk to him. I promise I won't mention your situation. I just want to feel him out about his attitude toward you and see if he'd make a decent guardian."

"I can't do that."

Caleb was looking irritated, but what more could she say? If he wouldn't help her, any hope she'd had would be gone.

"Okay, what about this," Caleb leaned forward again. "What if I could find a good home to place the baby in until your release?"

"My mother would still be chosen over strangers. God, I wish she'd never found out I was pregnant. For some stupid reason, the authorities informed her of my arrest, and then let it slip."

"Would it really be so bad if the baby stayed with her for a little while?"

"Yes!" Leah looked around to the guard again and got a warning glare. "I can't let that happen. This baby is not going to grow up the way I did. It would be better off being raised by a family of apes."

"Your letter said a life depends on me. Please, tell me what I can do to help you."

"I need you to prove my mother is unfit. You do that kind of thing in your business, don't you? I need you to help me fight her on this before the baby is born. The paper said your friend, the man who died, was an investigator for your firm. Have her investigated."

"Okay, I can do that. In the meantime, I'll see if I can find a way to get you out of here." Caleb took a deep breath looking somewhat content. "How much time do I have before the baby is born?"

"Not much."

"Give me a number, Leah. Are we talking a month, two months?"

"Umm, probably closer to a few weeks."

Chapter Two

Bogdan Petrov leaned his head back and closed his eyes. He took a long draw from his cigar, letting the sweet smelling smoke slide through his lips and climb to his nose. Like the rest of the furniture in the house, the overstuffed chair was covered in a heavy floral print. It looked ridiculous. It was a perfect match for the woman who lived here. But, what did it matter? It would all be replaced soon.

As long as his plans moved smoothly, he'd have enough money to live the way he had before going to prison. And, like before, he'd succeed on his own.

It hadn't been easy, staying independent. He'd had to negotiate a deal with a crime organization in Russia. They owned the largest private sex club in Moscow called L'vov Logovo, or in English: The Lions Lair. The club served as a cover for the organization of the same name. He'd paid a high price to buy his cousin out of slavery to them. The club's manager, Adrik Sokolov, also known as The Ghost, hadn't been happy about losing her to an outsider, even though she was his cousin.

Since bringing her to America, Katya had been his right hand—loyal, and reliable. She'd even helped him obtain a position to appease his parole officer and get him closer to his target. The weekly paycheck was an insult. But the situation had given him power over the

Fletcher girl and now her condition strengthened that power.

Leannette Fletcher was exactly where he wanted her, desperate and afraid. She'd have to pay for the sins of her father, for the theft of his money, and causing his humiliating and inconvenient incarceration. Petrov had lost almost everything from his past. The only possessions he still owned were a small, outdated wardrobe and his prized music boxes.

He opened one of his favorites, a silver powder box that played a Viennese waltz. The tinkling music soothed his nerves. Thank heaven Katya had packed them for safekeeping when she heard he'd been arrested.

Inside the lid was a mirror. Petrov checked to make sure every jet-black hair in his neatly trimmed goatee was in place. A man's appearance was the keystone to his power.

"Boggy, honey, are you smoking one of those nasty cigars again?"

Petrov snapped the box shut. His quiet moment had been spoiled.

His new bride, Peggy, staggered in after sleeping until ten. Her satin robe barely held together over a threadbare, black teddy she must have bought in the seventies. Her bleached hair stood on end. Her makeup from the day before made her look like a fresh painting that had been left out in the rain. She tried for a youthful appearance that only caused her to seem much older than her forty-five years.

He watched as she poured vodka over a short glass of ice. That and a few pills were her usual breakfast. She would be replaced soon, as well. For now, she was necessary.

"If you'd rather I smoke away from the house I could accommodate you, *milachka*," he replied calmly, although she wasn't dear to him at all. "But, I couldn't say when I'd return."

"Don't say that, honey. It's been so long since I've had a man to take care of. I love seeing you here in my daddy's old study."

An endearment in his native tongue always succeeded in turning her to pudding. A subtle threat didn't hurt either.

"Your father left you a nice house and you don't take any better care of it than you do yourself." He held back a smile as Peggy nervously straightened her robe and fingered her hair into a more managed mess. "I don't see why my cigars would be a problem."

"Oh, I don't really mind them, sweetie. I guess I just woke up feeling a little grumpy. I'm sorry. As soon as I'm dressed, I'll come straighten this room out. I'm not used to taking care of the house on my own. My daughter always helped me. Who would have thought she'd end up being a common criminal like her father?"

Petrov turned to hide his smile. "Don't be too harsh, my dear. Sometimes bad things happen to nice people."

****

Thoughts spun through Caleb's mind like leaves in a tornado. The sweet, innocent girl he'd been longing for was in jail. *Had she ever been in trouble before? She was pregnant. How many men had she taken home with her the way she had him? Who was the baby's father? She was pregnant. Why wouldn't she want her mother at a time like this? Had she been involved with the robbery? Who would want to set her up for the crime, and why? She was pregnant. He couldn't be involved with a pregnant woman. She was having a baby, for heaven's sake. He couldn't be around a baby. But, he had to help her.*

Caleb could count on his best friend and investigator, Ted Newsome, to dig up any dirt on Leah's mom. Ted was the best in his field. Caleb patted his pocket where he'd put the information on Margaret Fletcher. He'd memorized all Leah told him and written it down before he left the jail parking lot. He also intended to get a few answers about Leah.

When he pulled into the parking garage, Caleb could barely remember the trip from the jail. His mind had snapped back to his immediate surroundings when the sound of his car's engine echoed off the stone walls and pillars around him.

Parking garages tended to paralyze him with fear. Several years ago his twin brother, Connor, had been attacked while leaving work one night. He'd been robbed and left permanently disfigured and nearly dead. Caleb had almost lost Connor that day. On an emotional level it had about killed him as well. No one could really understand the bond between twins unless they were one.

He rushed to the elevator, heart pounding, palms sweating. Damn, he felt like the biggest sissy ever. Why did they have to work in a building that sat on a freaking parking garage?

"How was your morning, Mr. Caleb?" Ruth Ann waited at the elevator doors with a cup of coffee in one hand and a blueberry muffin in the other. Sugar and caffeine were just what the doctor ordered.

"I've come to the conclusion that you're psychic, Ruth Ann. There's no other explanation for the way you're able to track me. If I'm ever lost in a blizzard, you're the woman I want to lead the search and rescue team." He sipped the strong, black coffee. Ruth Ann had made his first cup twenty-five years ago when she'd been newly hired. It had been a father and son day at the office and she'd wanted Connor and him to have the full experience. "As for your question, my morning was interesting. Could you please call and ask Ted to come by my office?"

"I'd be delighted. And, if we ever have a blizzard in Florida, I'll be first on the dog sled to come find you." Ruth Ann returned to her desk where a canvas bag sat overflowing with delicate white yarn and two long needles.

"What do you have here?" Caleb pointed at the bag. It amazed him how Ruth Ann could answer phones, file, run errands, and a million other tasks while knitting a blanket in a week.

"Lisa is expecting another baby this fall." Ruth Ann raised the needles from the bag to show a tiny sweater hanging from them.

Caleb had known all four of Ruth Ann's daughters when they were growing up. Since then, they'd given her about a hundred grandchildren. At least that was his estimation.

Caleb swallowed hard. The sweater looked so delicate. Angel had never had the chance to wear anything like that. It would have been so beautiful on her.

He looked away abruptly. He needed to change the subject.

"I didn't see my father this morning before I left. I'm sure he and my mom must have gotten back to town by now."

"As a matter of fact, I was supposed to call him as soon as you walked through the door. He plans to corner you in your office with his Monday morning moodiness. I decided to let you have coffee first." Ruth Ann tucked the knitting back into her bag. "I'm sorry if I…"

"No worries." Caleb knew she was distressed about bringing up a bad memory with her knitting project. His emotions must have shown on his face. He pecked a kiss on her cheek before heading to his office.

Obviously, Ruth Ann hadn't been needed to call his father. Ian McCrae was holding court behind Caleb's desk for a couple of female paralegals. They were cooing over pictures of the newest McCrae member, baby Cole.

"If you'll excuse us, ladies, I need to speak to my son for a moment." Ian scooped up the pictures as the women left the room. They nodded on their way out, but Caleb knew they didn't care much for him. He'd heard a rumor they referred to him as the Ice Prince. "Have a seat, Caleb, we need to talk."

"My chair seems to be occupied." Caleb stayed standing by the door with his arms crossed. Ian rolled his eyes and moved to the other side of the desk.

"You need an attitude adjustment, son." Ian shoved the baby pictures into his jacket pocket. "You have a light workload right now, no court appearances until next month. I want you to take some time off. Get your head together. Straighten out your priorities."

"My priorities are right here, Dad. And, my head is

just fine."

"Really?" Ian folded his arms on the desk and leaned forward. "Where was your head when you walked out of Jordan's hospital room? It was the proudest moment of your brother's life and you didn't even glance at the baby. We've always made family our first priority. That's why we chose to practice family law."

"You made that choice long before we entered law school," Caleb shot back. "Besides that, Connor understands how I feel."

"Gee, I'm glad he does. I certainly don't." Ian leaned back. "It's been six years. You need to get over this. I think you left therapy too soon."

"I'm not going back into therapy. Those doctors don't understand any better than you do."

A tap on the door ended the conversation. However, Caleb's mood didn't improve when Ted walked in pushing his eight-month-old son in a stroller.

"Sorry, I had to bring JT along," Ted shrugged. "I was at the doctor's office with Jenny when Ruth Ann called."

"Is Jenny sick?" His father knelt beside the stroller to tickle the baby's belly.

A surge of guilt washed over Caleb. He'd been a great father, always involved in their activities. Now he longed for the next generation.

"Only in the mornings, so far." Ted grinned and winked. "It seems that this little guy is going to be a big brother in about seven months.

"You need to find a new hobby, Ted." Ian laughed. "I'll take JT for a walk while the two of you talk."

Caleb shook Ted's hand and congratulated him

before they sat to discuss business. He gave Ted the information on Margaret Fletcher that Leah had provided. He also gave a rundown on Leah's situation.

"There's a reason the girl doesn't want to hand her baby over to this woman," Ted said. "I'll find out everything I can. I'll also put my ear to the ground and see if I can come up with something on that robbery. Are you absolutely sure she wasn't involved?"

"No I'm not, but I just can't see Leah getting into that kind of trouble. She's too smart for that. See if you can get the police report and court transcripts on her case."

"I'll get right on it, Cal."

Chapter Three

Leah lay on the exam table, her feet in the stirrups. It was awkward and uncomfortable, but she'd gotten used to it. Instead of thinking about fields of wildflowers or a remote country cottage, she thought about Caleb. He'd introduced himself as Cal, when they first met. He still looked every bit as handsome as she remembered, even better in a suit and tie. He was definitely not the kind of man who'd be interested in a woman with a felony record.

It must have horrified him to find himself on the other side of a jail visitor's booth from a past one-night stand. After seeing the condition she was in, she doubted he'd be in the market for a repeat of that performance. As wonderful as it had been, casual sex wasn't her style. Look at the way this one turned out. Months later she was still fantasizing about him. Oh, the things he'd done to her.

"I'm such a ninny," her mother would say. "Why do I fall for every good-looking man who crosses my path?"

Was she turning into her mother?

"Ouch!"

"Sorry." The doctor snapped off his gloves and threw them into the red plastic trash bag. "It looks like everything's going as planned. You've dilated almost two centimeters and your cervix is thinning."

"Believe me, doc, I didn't plan any of this."

"Be that as it may, the staff will be ready to transport you to the hospital whenever you're ready. I'll see you next week, if not sooner."

The newest guard glared at her from a chair by the door as she dressed. Even though she'd just hired on a few weeks ago, Katya Lebedev was the toughest corrections officer on the staff. She was super model tall and beautiful, but acid ran through her veins. On her first day she'd been talked back to by one of the most butch inmates. Two minutes later, Katya walked out of the woman's cell with a bloody nightstick and not a hair out of place. The prisoner was missing all eight front teeth. Katya claimed the woman slipped and hit her mouth on the end of her bunk. Leah hated being left alone with her.

"Be sure to get plenty of rest tonight, Tinkerbelle," Katya instructed with her light accent. "You have a big day tomorrow."

"My days are all pretty much the same in this place," Leah replied.

"Not tomorrow. Tomorrow, you'll have a very important visitor."

"The only person on my visitor list is my attorney and he was just here. I don't expect him to return for at least a few days."

"I've added another name." Katya gripped her arm as she guided her down the corridor. "Someone wants to speak to you regarding important business."

"How do you know that?" A chill ran up Leah's spine. "Who is this person?"

Katya clanged the cell door loudly between them before she responded. "The Russian is coming to see you," she cooed. "You'd better cooperate with him or you'll answer to me."

As the guard's twittering laugh faded down the hallway, Leah recalled the last time she spoke to her father.

She'd been fifteen when she walked past her parents' room and caught him hastily stuffing clothes into a duffel bag. He refused to say where he was going, but insisted she listen to him carefully. "Leah, if you see a big Russian with a little black beard, you must run and hide. That man will do anything to get at me. He might even try to use you. I crossed him up and he's going to want to get even." Before running out the door he added, "I swear he'll be the death of me."

Her father's body was found in a retention pond two days later. He'd been beaten to death. She'd always assumed that his prediction regarding the Russian had come true.

****

To prove to his father that he was putting his family first, Caleb invited his mother to lunch at an open-air café on the waterfront.

Melly McCrae had been raised on Florida beaches and still embraced a more Bohemian lifestyle than her suit and tie husband. They had a yin and yang relationship that worked better than most. Caleb and Connor had grown up studying for the bar during the week and windsurfing on weekends. It was the best of both worlds.

His mother talked about the Independence Day festival she was planning with the Bay Area Women's Club to raise money for a new playground while they ate cold crab salad. After the plates were taken away the conversation changed.

"You have to see what I picked up for little Cole at the surf shop." Melly searched several cloth shopping bags before holding up a tiny pair of Hawaiian print board shorts.

"I don't suppose you have a miniature boogie board in there somewhere, do you?"

"No." She sighed. "The sales person said I should wait until he can swim well. I'll go back for that in a few months."

"I'm surprised you haven't had a ski boat sent down for him."

"All in good time. I did have a full set of nursery furniture shipped, now that we know he's strong and healthy."

Caleb's chest tightened. "You mean, now that you know he'll survive."

"Well, yes." Melly put the shorts back in the bag and took a sip of mint tea. "It's a fact of life we've been unfortunate enough to learn."

"I guess you and Dad have discussed my supposed need of therapy."

"Honey, your reaction to the new baby proved you still have issues to work through. What could it hurt to talk to someone?"

"Find me a shrink who has held his child while she died after watching her mother's body butchered on wet pavement. Oh, and don't forget to make sure he was responsible for the incident that killed her."

"You were not responsible." Tears gathered in Melly's eyes. "The inquest deemed it an accident."

"Someone was responsible for it and I was the guy behind the wheel."

"Caleb, sometimes an accident is just an accident." She located a tissue in her handbag. "I love you, son. I can't stand to watch you only living half your life."

"What does that mean?"

"You need balance, good times to counter the bad, and a home life to equal your work life." She sniffed and dabbed her eyes.

"Let me get this straight. I should find my own bachelor pad and party like a rock star. That'll fix everything. I'll forget all about my daughter."

"I can't do this any more, Caleb." Melly stood and gathered her shopping bags. "Let me know when you're ready to end your pity party."

Caleb mentally kicked his own ass all the way back to the office. His mom was the happiest, most supportive person he knew and he'd made her cry. Maybe his dad was right and he should take a little time off. Perhaps he should even follow Connor's lead and start another branch of the family firm in a different town. He could make a whole new start. It had certainly worked for Connor. He'd barely had a chance to sit in his desk chair before his cell phone rang.

"How's it goin', boss?"

"Not bad, how 'bout you?" Caleb always cringed when Ted called him boss, but it seemed to be a habit.

"I'm doing great! I'm headed to the office now and wanted to make sure you'd be there. You'd better have your reading glasses handy. While I was interviewing the Fletcher's neighbors, my friend at the courthouse put together a shit-ton of stuff you won't believe. It seems your girlfriend isn't the first in her family to see the backside of jail bars."

Caleb was surprised by his feeling of

disappointment. He knew Leah lived in a rundown, lower income area. He understood that she worked in a questionable establishment. But, he'd thought it was a matter of being young and trying to get started. He hadn't expected it to be an inherited way of life. He'd hoped the incident she was jailed for was a fluke that would eventually be straightened out.

"How soon will you be here?"

He didn't want to hear anything more over the phone. "I'm pulling into the garage now. Give me a minute to park and I'll be right up.

"Damn! Can you believe a guy just passed me on the ramp? It looks like he's stopping at the gate. What the hell?"

"Stay in your car, Ted. Lock the doors."

Ted wasn't listening. He was shouting a distance from the phone. "Hey! You guys can't park there. What's going on?" Two car doors slammed then all hell broke loose. After a cacophony of loud bangs and crashes, the phone went silent.

"Call 911," Caleb yelled. He ran past Ruth Ann's desk. "Ted is being attacked at the entrance to the parking garage. It sounded like at least two men."

He didn't wait for the elevator. With all the adrenaline pumping through his body four flights of stairs seemed like rolling out of bed. He couldn't let Ted suffer the way his brother had. *Please, God, don't let me be too late.*

He hadn't been there for Connor. He was too late for John, their former investigator and friend. He'd been useless to Brenda, his fiancée; and Angel, his daughter. He couldn't let down his best friend too.

Near the entrance to the garage, Caleb saw the rear

of an old, black, Buick La Sabre race toward the street. Its license plate was obscured with mud.

Ted lay on the concrete, one leg still inside the car. The area around Ted's left eye had already started to swell and darken. Blood ran from his nose and busted lip. He gripped his arms around his ribs and breathed in shallow pants. "Hey, Cal," he whispered, grinning with bloody teeth. "You mind parking my car for me?"

"Shut up, asshole." Caleb felt weak with relief. He reached inside the car for a leather bag to use as a cushion under Ted's head. "Do you know who did this to you?"

"Two guys I've never seen before. Big like linebackers. Talked funny...like Boris."

"Boris?"

"You know." Ted's eyes looked glassy. "On Bullwinkle. They said...don't be nosy...don't ask questions." He chuckled, which sounded more like a gurgle. "That's my job, man."

Caleb hadn't realized that a small crowd from inside the building had gathered behind him until Ian knelt by Ted's head. "I'll pick up Jenny. We'll meet you at the hospital. And I'll call Melly. She and Miss Hannah can keep your son at our house as long as you need."

Caleb held back a groan. The last thing he needed was a baby around the house. He instantly felt guilty. Ted would do anything for them, including getting himself beaten half to death for information they needed.

"Wait, Ian." Ted's expression became deadly serious. "Don't let Jenny get upset...the pregnancy."

"Don't worry, Ted." Ian smoothed his hair back

like he was his own son. "I'll tell her you stubbed your toe."

"Move back and let us get to work here, gentlemen." Emergency medics had arrived.

Caleb told the police what he heard over the phone and what Ted said when he arrived. They were anxious to question Ted, but would have to wait for the doctor's okay.

After the ambulance loaded the gurney and pulled away, Caleb leaned down to pick up the leather bag Ted used as a pillow. It was the bag Ted used for his notes and documents. He'd take it to the hospital and read what the contact at the courthouse had found. Did it have anything to do with this attack? Patting his pockets, he realized he left his keys in the office.

"How bad is it?" Ruth Ann asked when he returned.

"He's been beaten up pretty good, but it's fixable."

"Was he able to say who attacked him?"

"Boris," Caleb chuckled. "Have you ever heard of Boris and Bullwinkle?"

"That boy and his classic cartoons," Ruth Ann shook her head. "Bullwinkle was a moose who hung out with a flying squirrel named Rocky. Boris Badenov was a villain on the show."

"Boris Badenov, seriously?"

"I know, it was silly, but it was a cartoon," she laughed. "He was supposed to be a Russian spy. The show was made during the cold war. The term, *politically correct*, hadn't been coined yet. People thought all bad guys were Russian and all Russians were spies. I'm so glad we've moved past that now."

The cold war might be over, but Caleb had a

feeling his troubles had just started with a couple of Russians.

Chapter Four

Tampa General had been busy all night. Caleb spent a few hours reading about Leah's history. Margaret, a.k.a. Peggy Fletcher, had lived at the same address all her life, inheriting the Victorian monstrosity from her parents after they died twenty years ago. According to her neighbors, she was a sloppy, pitiful drunk who popped pills like M&Ms. She hadn't driven a car since hers was pulled out of a koi pond at the local Chinese steakhouse. She had booze delivered regularly and often roamed around her yard at night crying in her robe and slippers. A man had moved into the house recently. He seemed to be on the anti-social side, but was able to keep Peggy indoors when he was home. Mother of the year, she was not. Caleb had seen worse in his family law experience, but he understood why Leah didn't want to hand her baby over to this woman.

Thinking about Leah made his heart feel like lead. He hadn't been able to get her off his mind for the last eight months. He'd become obsessed with finding her. Now, everything had changed. She was a package deal. A package he couldn't handle. He owed it to her to help, though. She'd made a tremendous emotional impact on him in just one night. Then, he'd left her without a word.

There was a court file in the bag with the name Charles Fletcher written across the tab. His rap sheet listed a series of non-violent, petty crime spanning twenty years. There'd probably been more in a juvenile record that was now sealed. He'd started with pickpocketing and purse snatching. Then, he graduated to auto theft and B&E/burglary.

He grew up in the same Ybor City neighborhood as Peggy Fletcher and after marriage, he'd moved into her family home. His occupation was freelance party clown, which would be impossible to track. Along the edge of the paper was a handwritten note, *good at picking locks and cracking small safes*. Hmm, something extra in his bag of tricks.

The last entry was twelve years old and the most interesting. He'd been arrested for burgling a house in an upscale area and stealing a small collection of antique music boxes. Evidence showed a safe in the house had been cracked, but the owner refused to state what had been inside. It must have been something he'd been hiding. The next items in the file were newspaper clippings attached with a paperclip. This cop had been thorough. First was the story of the break-in, followed by Fletcher's arrest. Next was news that he'd been released after a meeting with the prosecutor. He obviously made some sort of deal. The final article was about the discovery of Charles' body. Damn! Caleb hadn't expected that. The last item in the package was a copy of the autopsy report. He'd been bludgeoned beyond recognition sending shards of rib bone through a few vital organs, and then he'd been dumped in a retention pond.

Caleb made a note in his phone to find out what happened in the trial regarding the last burglary. He hadn't realized music boxes were such a hot item, but surely it had something to do with Charlie's murder. After all, how many enemies could a clown have?

What had it been like for Leah to grow up knowing something like that? She must have been in her teens at the time. Was she close to her father? She'd certainly followed his footsteps to the jailhouse. That led to the question of her innocence. Had she taken a page from the old man's book? Maybe he'd been grooming her to work the family business. It was no wonder she'd worked in a male dominated environment and taken home one-night stands. She probably had daddy issues. Her mother wouldn't have been any help.

Caleb looked up when he heard his father enter the room.

"Jenny just came out for a minute." Ian handed him a cup of coffee. "They've taped Ted's ribs and stitched him up. He must have hit his head, though. They suspect a concussion and plan to keep him overnight. He's being moved to a room now."

Caleb nodded. He could tell by the grim expression his father wore, they were thinking the same thing. Losing John last year had been like losing a favorite uncle. He'd been investigating a case for Connor and his wife when Jordan's psycho ex-husband knifed him in the woods and hung his body from a tree in their backyard. Ted had named his son, JT, John Theodore, after him. Connor's son Cole was named Coleman after a close friend of Jordan's family, but had the middle name John.

It was John's obituary that had led Leah to him. It was the only positive thing that had come from the tragedy…or was it positive? Ted had been asking questions about the Fletchers. His attackers had told him to mind his own business.

****

Leah Fletcher cocooned herself in a thin blanket at the back of the lower bunk. She'd hung her pillowcase at the end of the bed frame to block the glare from the common area. It was hard to sleep with the security lights burning.

"Take that drape down, or I'll come in there and take it away from you," the nightshift guard hissed as she tapped the bars with her nightstick, "I want to see everything going on in there."

"The light shines straight into my eyes." Leah sat up and, with a single jerk, tore the barrier down. "Can I at least sleep at the other end of the bed?"

"No. I want to see your face when I walk by. Now, get some sleep."

As soon as the guard's hard soled shoes clomped out of hearing range, Leah realized her cellmate had stopped snoring…damn!

"Did you enjoy that, Tinkerbelle?" Rosie's head hung down from the side of the top bunk. "You know how much I hate attention over here and you sure as hell know how much I hate being woke up."

Leah didn't appreciate the nickname her cellmate had given her, but she didn't complain. Not much was known about Rosie Washington. She'd never shared why she was there or anything about her life outside the jail. One thing Leah had heard was that Rosie was often referred to as Rottweiler. She'd been told Rosie had a habit of biting until she drew blood when she fought. So far she hadn't seen firsthand proof of that claim and didn't want to.

Rosie was a tall, statuesque, African-American

with perfect caramel skin tone framed by hundreds of long braids. Despite her abrasive attitude, she started and ended every day reading from a bible and silently praying. Most of the time they spent alone was in silence. Leah didn't ask questions and stayed to herself. They quietly coexisted, but Rosie had told her on her first day in the cell they'd never be friends. She didn't associate with criminals.

"Sorry, Rosie."

Leah listened to the soft sounds of shifting bunks, shuffling feet, and grumbling voices down the walkway. The aroma of meatloaf and creamed corn lingered from the nearby cafeteria. She prayed exhaustion would send her to sleep before the sun came up.

If she was lucky she'd be out in two months—if not, it'd be another five. Either way, it would be too late. She hoped with all her heart Caleb would come through. Seeing him today didn't help her exhaustion.

Memories of the night they spent together played through her mind. He wasn't the gentlest lover she'd ever had, but he was thrilling. He kissed and held her like he never wanted to let go. He kept a silent, fevered pace to escape inside her. Every touch of his hands, mouth, and body was a desperate plea for something more, but she didn't know what. All she did know was that he clung to her like a drowning man to an outstretched branch. Then, he left without a word.

Today he seemed cold, distant, and judgmental. What had she expected?

Chapter Five

Petrov was annoyed by the process of passing through the jail gate, but from there it was easy. His cousin was on the inside to pave the way.

Most people would call Katya a ball buster, but what did he care? She was on his side. Those who knew them showed her as much respect as they did him. The others who hadn't been as courteous wished they had. She was ruthless, resourceful, and beautiful. They'd grown up together. She understood him.

Katya met him at the entrance to act as his escort. Her manner was as stiff as the uniform she wore. She didn't say a word until they'd stopped in the empty corridor outside the booth area.

"There will be an officer at the wall behind her. He's there to make sure she behaves. He cannot hear your side of the conversation." Petrov loved that Katya still spoke with the accent of their homeland. "I warn you, though, the conversation is recorded. If there is an incident, they may decide to listen to it later."

"That shouldn't be a problem, *babochka*. You've told her not to cross me, haven't you?" He called her butterfly because her skin was as delicate as dragonfly wings. He used a fingertip to trace her only imperfection, a scar on the left side of her neck. It had been caused by the one and only time she defied him.

"Please, Bogdan." She jumped back and glanced at

a camera on the wall above the door. "They watch our every move."

He stepped closer, hiding the hand that caught hers from the camera's view. He curled her little finger in his grip, squeezing it almost to the point of breaking. "I'm waiting for an answer to my question."

"I told her to tell you all you want to know," she hissed.

"That's good." He let her hand drop. "It would have been perfect if you'd arranged for me to meet with her without glass and recording devices. I expect you to destroy the tape of our conversation before you leave here today. Even better, you should bring it to me. That way I'll know it was disposed of properly."

"But Bogdan—"

Petrov froze her next words with an icy stare.

****

"You!" Leah gasped.

"Yes, Ms. Fletcher, it is me, Bogdan Petrov." He wore the smile of an eight-year-old boy with a spider caught under his cup. "We've never had a chance to speak to one another, but I thought you might recognize me."

"You're the new manager of the Blue Moon. I remember when you took over. It was just a short time before I left."

The dark, well dressed, man occasionally walked through the club and straight to the offices in the back. She'd never heard him speak and wasn't aware of his accent. There was one thing she had noticed though: he would send for a drink to be delivered by a dancer rather than a waitress. She didn't mind not being among the chosen. The dancer he requested wouldn't be seen for a while, then she'd dress and scurry to her car like a scared mouse. Most of the time, she never returned. "Why are you here? I already assumed I'd lost my job. It doesn't seem reasonable that you'd come all this way to give me that news."

"I'd never fire you, *Golubshka*. That means little dove in my homeland. Your job is safe." His smile broadened as he leaned closer to the glass partition. "You don't even realize what a large role I play in your life. I've been waiting for years to get close to you."

"I don't understand," Leah admitted. "I haven't known you for years. I don't really know you now. And, I'm not anyone's little dove."

"But, I knew you." Petrov said. "Your father and I played chess several times a week. He was an idiot, but he played chess well. He never stayed past three o'clock. *I have to see my little girl safely home*, he would say. Do you remember? That was when he would meet you at the high school and walk you home. I sometimes followed and watched. You weren't a little girl. You were an alluring young woman. I knew one day you'd be as beautiful as you are now. Even in your current condition you emit an innocent sensuality that's hard to resist."

"You knew my father?"

"Of course. He worked for me—he stole things for me—and he stole something *from* me, too. That's why he had to die and that's what brings me to you. He wouldn't tell me where he hidden my money, but he had to have given it to you. He didn't care for anyone but you."

"My father left us with nothing." Leah's voice only raised an octave or two, but the guard behind her cleared his throat. "I work every day to pay the bills and buy food. The money my mother lives on now is what I managed to save with no help from anyone."

"Good show." Petrov softly chuckled. "Such a poor little girl. No one would know you're concealing almost a million untaxed dollars."

"A million?" Leah sucked in a gasp that nearly choked her. "My father never came close to that kind of money."

"Nine-hundred-and-twenty-thousand to be exact," Petrov smirked. "I've been over every inch of your apartment and the rest of your mother's property. I haven't found it yet, but I promise you I will. I want that money. I don't need it. I have ways of getting everything I desire, but, this is a matter of principle. I spent ten years in prison for that robbery. The money belongs to me."

"You said you searched my mother's property. How can that be?"

"It was the only reasonable place to look." Petrov sighed. "Like I said, your father was an idiot. He'd leave it in an easy place for you to find or you would have hidden it there yourself."

"If you've hurt my mother, I'll kill you," Leah whispered.

"Ha! I haven't hurt her, my *Golubshka*, I married her. Like I said, we're family now. I even agreed to turn the room next to ours into a nursery for the baby. She's looking forward to bringing the little one home. That child you carry will be mine unless I get what I want. Your lawyer friend won't interfere. I've already sent him a message."

What did he mean by that? What message? How

did he know about Caleb? And, what was this monster doing with her mother? Anxiety cramped her stomach.

"Your mother is happy now. She and your baby will stay that way as long as I get my money." He moved closer again. "Just tell me where it is, Leah."

"You don't understand! My father didn't leave anything. I don't have your money."

"I see." Petrov's gave her a wicked sneer. "You need a little more time to think about it. I can arrange that." He hung the phone receiver back on its cradle and left without a glance back.

****

"His name is Bogdan Petrov." Caleb buttoned Ted's shirt as he listened to the information. Caleb had suffered broken ribs after his accident six years ago and knew how painful every movement could be. "Fletcher turned on him. He told the cops where the handoff would be made and they caught it all on surveillance video. Even though Fletcher was killed soon after, they didn't need his testimony to convict Petrov. He finished serving ten of a fifteen year sentence almost a year ago."

"I know he's behind this," Caleb reasoned. "But, why wait so long? And, what does any of this have to do with Leah?"

"I imagine he used some of the past few months gathering his associates and making plans." Ted groaned as he slid off the edge of the bed and stood. "We know he has at least two blockheads working for him."

Jenny raced into the room and handed her son to Caleb. "You shouldn't be walking around on your own yet! I'll have the nurse bring in a wheelchair. Watch JT for just a minute. I forgot to bring the stroller."

Caleb held the eight-month-old boy as far from his body as his arms would stretch. According to the watery grin on his face, the baby didn't seem to mind, but Caleb was seconds from a full-blown panic attack. It must have been evident to Ted as well.

"Walk toward me and set the baby on the bed. All we have to do is make sure he doesn't fall off."

Caleb followed Ted's instructions, feeling as stiff as a wooden Indian. The baby rolled back on the pillow and giggled.

"Thanks for not tossing my son on the floor." Ted sighed with relief. "Jenny doesn't know about…everything. She didn't mean any harm."

"It's not her fault. I just…I can't. I know it's stupid."

"If you recall, you were that way about all kids for a long time. When you met your niece, Lizzy, she worked her magic on you and you could barely let her out of your sight. Maybe a baby will come along one day that does the same thing for you."

"I doubt that. You didn't see the way I nearly freaked out just being in the same room with Connor's son. It does remind me of another small problem though. If I'm successful in keeping Leah's baby from her mother, I have to find a place for it to stay until she gets out of jail. She doesn't want it to go to foster care. Do you think you and Jenny would be up for the job?"

"Man, I'd do anything for you, you know that. But, I have to turn you down. Jenny is in her first trimester and JT is almost more than she can handle."

"I understand that. I remember when Brenda…" Jenny followed a nurse with a wheelchair into the room.

"Is everything okay?"

"Yeah." Caleb cleared his throat. "I have to go. I'll see you guys later."

He was thankful for the interruption. Why had he brought up his late fiancée? He hadn't talked to anyone about Brenda since leaving therapy. No, that wasn't exactly true. He'd told his brother everything. Letting it all out without being judged had done more good than any of the doctors he'd spoken to. And Connor hadn't said the words he'd come to hate: *You should move on. You'll get over it.*

Chapter Six

"What's going on with you?" Rosie stepped beside Leah as they left the showers.

Leah wasn't used to being approached by her cellmate. As far as she knew, Rosie would just as soon see Leah floating facedown in an alligator infested canal than speak to her.

When Leah's only answer was a shrug, Rosie grabbed her collar and pulled her to the back of the line. "That Barbie-from-hell guard is paying an awful lot of attention to our little corner of heaven, Tinkerbelle."

"I don't know what to tell you, Rosie." Leah scanned the hallway to make sure no one was watching, and moved closer to whisper, "It's like a jigsaw puzzle with a few pieces missing. Katya is involved with a Russian man who's giving me a hard time, but I'm not sure what their connection is. She could be his lover, relative, employee, but she definitely takes her orders from him."

"Some guy here at the jail is giving you a hard time?" Rosie huffed. "What does he want? Is he one of those pregnancy pervs?"

"No, he runs a night club. I guess they get together outside the jail. He seems to have a lot of influence over her. It's a long story, but he says I have money that belongs to him. I don't have any money. If I did, I could have hired an attorney. He admitted to killing my father and I'm beginning to think he may have arranged the evidence that got me locked up here. He was my boss at the club and now he says he's married to my mother. He's even threatening to take my baby."

"Are you sure you're not just paranoid? Maybe it's that pregnancy hormone shit." Rosie shook her head as they rounded the last corner. "None of this makes any sense."

"Stop talking back there!"

Leah and Rosie snapped their heads up to see the cell doors wide open and the other inmates standing along the walkway looking nervous. Extra guards were moving inside several cells at one time. They seemed to be conducting a search.

Leah was the first to reach their door. On a gasp she fell back. She might have slumped to the floor if Rosie hadn't been close enough to block her fall. It was just like the raid on her apartment. Her upturned mattress revealed several books, toiletry items, personal letters, and pictures—none belonging to her. She'd never seen them before this moment.

"Well, well, well," Katya crooned to the two male guards behind her. "It looks like we've found our thief. I guess she hasn't learned anything from her punishment. She may have to be our guest for quite a while longer."

"You bitch!" One of the meanest inmates from a Latino gang tried to push her way inside. She shook a finger at Leah. "You stole the pictures of my kids!"

"She's got my private letters from my boyfriend!" another shouted. "She ain't gonna make it to the warden's office. I'm gonna kick her ass!"

"You can try kickin' my ass, puta." Rosie stayed

between Leah and the door. "I'm the one who took that shit."

"No, Rosie!" Leah knew neither of them was guilty. She'd been set up again. The Russian had come through on his threat.

"It's Fletcher's bunk. She's the one we're taking." Katya informed the guards.

"I couldn't very well hide it under my own bunk." Rosie tugged on the worn metal links that exposed the underside of her mattress. "I told you, this stuff is mine. Tinkerbelle is too much of a coward to take anything."

"So why are you admitting it?" the first Latino girl asked. "You ain't never even told anybody why you're here."

"It's none of your fuckin' business why I'm here, but I'm not going to let them punish a pregnant woman for something she didn't do."

One male guard was handcuffing Rosie while the other cleared the way down the corridor.

"Don't think this is over, Tinkerbelle," Katya sneered. "The Russian gets what he wants…always."

****

Caleb was satisfied to see his influence with the jail officials had worked out for Leah. She was waiting for him at a table in an outdoor courtyard. The fence was high and topped with razor wire. That didn't keep the sun from coming through. She'd never shown signs of violence or attempted to escape, so they'd also agreed to leave off her shackles. She wasn't a dangerous criminal. Everything about Leah's incarceration seemed blown out of proportion. No one he'd talked to knew why. Someone with authority had to be calling the shots.

Leah's face was tipped up to soak in the sun, but her expression didn't convey enjoyment. She actually looked more stressed than on his first visit.

"What's wrong?" Caleb sat across from her and took her hands. The casual contact was allowed, but he didn't usually touch his clients. Leah wasn't his typical client though, was she? He'd spent an unforgettable night with her, and had thought about her ever since. Looking down at her small hands in his made him remember how they'd felt on his hot naked body. He'd been cold every day since. He hoped he'd be able to let her go when their visit was over.

"I'm in more trouble than you can help me with, Cal, but I don't know who else to turn to."

"What happened in the short time since I was here last? I hate to point out the obvious, but you've been under lock and key."

"It was like a rerun of the day I was arrested. Someone planted stolen items in my bunk while I was in the shower." Leah told him about the search and how Rosie had taken the blame to keep her from having time added to her sentence.

"Are you sure Rosie wasn't guilty of the thefts?" Caleb asked.

"I can't imagine Rosie taking anything that doesn't belong to her. She may be in trouble, she may even be the meanest person I've ever met, but she has integrity. None of those items were worth anything. They wouldn't hold any interest to anyone but their owners." Leah paused for a moment. "Rosie hasn't told anyone why she's here, but I know it's serious. From comments she's made I've gathered that she's awaiting trial and expects to be transferred to the state prison. She plans to live out the rest of her life there. Whatever she did, she had to have had a good reason. That's the kind of person she is. She's been in plenty of fights here, but I've never heard of her starting one. She's only defended herself. Still, she's done a good job of winning those fights, and now she's considered a hard-ass. I'm afraid the case against her will be made worse because of all that."

"I'll see what I can find out about Rosie," Caleb said. "But I'm more concerned about you. Hiding those items wasn't just a prank. Someone inside the jail is trying to get you into serious trouble."

"I have more to tell you…a lot more."

Leah told Caleb about the Russian's visit. She also told him about Katya Lebedev.

Much of it Caleb already knew, or suspected. The guard was a new threat. She had access to Leah when no one else was watching. Her latest trick hadn't worked because of Rosie. Would she retaliate against them both? It was clearly time to call in more favors.

Caleb watched Leah as she spoke. He'd met her in the blue strobe lights at the club. He'd seen her in the glow of his car's dashboard and the candles she lit at her apartment. More recently, she'd been under the glare of flickering, humming, fluorescent bulbs. This time, she was bathed in sunshine. The pink on her cheeks and nose proved this was where she belonged. He was reminded, once again, how truly stunning she was, so soft and innocent.

Suddenly a fold in her shirt made a definite leap.

"What the hell was that?" Caleb jumped back from the table so quickly his chair nearly fell backward.

"That was the baby." Leah rolled her eyes and

rubbed her belly. "It's trying to tunnel its way out, but it has a lousy escape plan."

"You're not going into labor, are you?" The possibility caused Caleb's stomach to roll.

"Of course not." Leah laughed. "This has been happening for a long time now. From what I've learned from books at the library, I should get plenty of notice before the grand finale. I still have a little more time."

"Do they offer birthing classes here? My brother and his wife took one."

"You mean the place where couples sit on pillows on the floor and learn to huff and puff their way through delivery. No, I don't have the cute outfits for that…and I doubt Rosie would agree to act as my labor coach."

Caleb thought about the involvement Connor and Ted had taken with bringing their children into the world. Leah shouldn't be alone when the time came.

"The father of that child should be here. It isn't fair that you haven't told him. And why do you keep referring to it as *it*. Don't you know if it's a boy or girl?"

"I get basic care here. That doesn't cover ultrasounds or sonograms. If you're so worried about it, you can assist in the delivery."

"Oh hell no!" Caleb nearly jumped from his seat. "It's not my baby!"

Leah squeezed her folded hands together and set her mouth into a firm straight line. Caleb's blood rushed through his veins and his head began to ache. "Look," he growled. "I'm not stupid. I know how to use a calendar and I can even count—this kid can't be mine."

"You sound so sure about that."

"Listen to me, Leah." Caleb took her hand again, forcing himself to hold it gently as panic built in his chest. "I've been there. I've done that. I wasn't any good at it. I never want to go through it again. No kid deserves me as a father."

"The chances are slim that it's yours. We were only together that one time." Leah studied their joined hands and shrugged. "It could be anybody's. I mean, with all the men I've taken home with me…I'm not sure I can even remember all their names." Leah looked him in the eye and took a deep breath. "All I know is that it's mine. I want it. I'll take care of it any way I have to. We'll be fine."

She reminded him of a fierce little lioness. She would be a great mother, and someday, a loving partner to a very lucky man. He regretted he couldn't be that man.

"Of course you will," he replied. "But, you have to be careful. I'll do what I can for Rosie. It seems like she has your back. My first priority is getting that Lebedev woman away from you, though. We have to make sure you're safe until we get you out of here."

"Visiting time is over," the guard announced.

They stood. Caleb took the one brief hug he was allowed at the end of a visit, something he'd never done before. When her firm, round belly touched him, memories flooded back—familiar longing, regret, and sadness. He wished he could wash away the last six years and start new memories with Leah. It was the first time he'd wished Angel had never existed…and he felt ashamed.

Chapter Seven

Katya opened her apartment door with one hand holding the top of her silk robe together. Petrov walked inside wearing a pleasant smile. He didn't want to alarm her. He settled into the overstuffed armchair she usually reserved for herself. She gave the small leather bag he set by his feet a curious glance, but knew better than to question him. The room was small, a little too warm, and smelled of strong, floral scented soap.

"You caught me by surprise, Bogdan. If you had called, I would have met you at your office. I could have at least been dressed." One hand fidgeted with her damp hair while the other still clasped her robe over her chest. "If you'll give me just a moment…"

"No. Stay here." Petrov pulled a comb from his inside pocket to run through his hair and beard, and then straightened the lapels of his jacket. "I'll only be a few minutes. I have a lot to do today."

"You must have come for the tape." Katya found her purse on the dinette table and rummaged inside to retrieve the cassette from his conversation with Leah. "If this is all you came for, I don't want to keep you from your other errands."

"Thank you for this, but it's not why I'm here. I came to talk to you." Petrov slid the tape into his pocket. "You're the only family I have left, little kitten. That's why I pulled you out of the hell of L'vov

Logovo and brought you to this country." He watched her face pale and knew she was mentally recalling her life as a slave in one of the most infamous, private sex clubs in Moscow. "I told you I would protect you as long as you did as I asked."

"I have," she blurted. "I've done my best."

"But, Leah wasn't blamed for the stolen items." Petrov shrugged. "Nothing happened to her at all. Is that your best, Katya?"

"That other bitch interfered."

"It was a simple task. You disappointed me." Petrov slid to the edge of his seat and leaned forward. "Do you remember what happened the last time you disappointed me?"

"You said you'd never lay a hand on me again. You promised." Katya's fingers went from her hair to the scar on her neck.

"I always keep my promises, but this morning I found out you've caused me more problems. This time, you must be punished."

Katya's eyes widened. "What have I done?" She was nearly as tough as him, and rarely showed fear. When she did, he found it exhilarating.

"You've been too public with your attention to Leah. People have noticed. They've talked about it. You're being assigned to a different position in the jail and put on probation. Her lawyer friend has arranged it all."

"But, they can't do that." Katya's hands began to shake. "You have the pictures of me with Judge Zeigler. He was supposed to take care of everything."

"It seems the judge has suddenly decided to retire. He left the country on an extended vacation. Can you see the difficult position you've put me in, my little butterfly?"

"What are you going to do to me?" Perspiration gathered on her upper lip.

"As you said, Katya, I promised not to harm you again. I'm simply going to leave you here to think about your life as it is now and how different it could be if I were to send you back to L'vov Logovo and The Ghost." Petrov drew a set of handcuffs from his bag and motioned her toward a support beam between her living room and kitchenette. "When I return this evening, you can cook dinner for me. Won't that be nice? We don't spend as much time together as we used to."

He pulled a ball gag from the bag. She tugged at the cuffs to find they only squeezed tighter. "That isn't necessary. Please don't."

"I'm afraid it is." Petrov fastened the gag in place. "I have friends coming to keep you company and I wouldn't want you to make a fuss and concern your neighbors." He produced a large black blindfold. She shook her head violently but he still managed to fasten around her head. "You see, my dear cousin, while you earned your punishment, they earned reward."

As soon as he'd secured Katya he opened the door to admit the two associates who'd taken care of warning the investigator. The first man, Carl, licked his lips as he walked toward her. The other, George, rubbed his hands together.

"Remember, my friends, I don't want a single mark left on her milky skin…at least not any that won't eventually fade, or you will suffer the same punishment." Then he added, "I'll look forward to dinner this evening, Katya. Don't forget to think about what I said."

****

Caleb sat in his father's study with a photo album in his lap. He'd run his hand over the cover several times, but hadn't collected the courage to open it. Why did he have the urge to look at Brenda's pictures? Just as he thought he'd begun to heal, all the bad memories had flooded back.

Seeing his brother's new baby, strong and healthy; remembering Angel's struggle in the short thirty minutes of her life; watching Leah touch her round belly protectively; picturing the crude roadside surgery that had removed his baby girl from her dead mother's body. Knowing the accident had been his fault no matter what the law said. There'd been no restitution to pay, no cure for his broken heart, no way to earn back his soul. Fingers of despair circled his throat and tightened. He couldn't breathe.

Like a miracle, his brother walked into the room.

Connor sat next to him and slid the album off his lap. When his hand touched Caleb's back, he couldn't stop himself. He grabbed Connor like a drowning man grabbing a branch. He held on tightly and let hot tears of anger and frustration fall.

"You're really here. Why are you here?" Caleb wiped a sleeve across his eyes and sank into the sofa. He was grateful that masculine embarrassment didn't exist between him and his twin.

"I'm just here for the day, but I can stay longer if you need me. I took a commuter flight to attend a deposition."

"There's no way I'd take you from your family."

"You're my family too, Cal." Connor walked to the wet bar and made them each a tall glass of ice water. "I've got some time to kill, if you need to talk."

"What I need to do is apologize. I let you down at the hospital when Cole was born."

"You didn't let me down, man. Damn, I could see how bad you were hurting."

"Aren't you going to jump on the bandwagon and tell me how I need to get over it?"

"Get over it?" Connor scoffed. "You'll never get over a thing like that any more than I'll get over what happened in that parking garage. We're both damned to our memories."

"So there's no hope."

"There's always hope." Connor rotated his glass and watched the ice swirl. "Angel and Brenda will be with you forever, but life moves on and you have to move with it. You have a right to be happy because you're a good person. They have a right to hold a brighter place in your heart. Don't keep making your memories of them something dark and tragic. They deserve better than that. You need to find a way to celebrate their lives rather than mourn them forever."

"How can I do that?"

"I can't give you all the answers, bro. Just keep your eyes open and an opportunity will come along."

As Connor took a long drink from his glass, Caleb studied the deep scar down his face. He recalled the damage that same incident had caused his brother's body. He'd been through his own hell and survived it. He was now a happy man with a family who loved him. He wasn't angry any more. If Connor could defeat his demons, maybe he could be happy someday too.

"So," Connor said in a lighter tone. "Ted tells me you have a girl."

"She's not my girl, she's my client."

"It sounds pretty complex for only being an acquaintance. I heard this incident has even caused a judge to resign."

Rumor was flooding the courthouse about Judge Ziegler's sudden resignation. Only Ted and the family knew it had happened mere hours after Leah's transcripts were requested.

"He was dirty," Caleb groused. "Besides that, Ted talks too much."

"Okay, now tell me about the girl."

Caleb gave his brother the *eat shit* stare, but Connor held fast to the smirk on his face. What the hell. He may as well spill it. "Do you remember the night you were arrested for the murder of that teenage girl, and then they thought I might be the killer? I said I'd been with a girl in Ybor City."

Caleb shrugged.

"Leah's the one I was with that night."

"That was last August. I'd call that a relationship."

"No, I didn't see her again until this week. It's complicated. She's in jail. Not exactly my favorite pickup spot."

"Yeah, but I hear she was set up. You're going to a lot of trouble to help her, so you must believe she didn't do it." Connor grasped his shoulder. "You know I'm here for you, Cal. You had our backs when Jordan's psycho ex-husband went on his rampage."

"I think I found a loophole to get her out of jail, but I don't see us together for the long haul."

"Why not?" Connor lifted both fists in a muscle

pose. "We come from good stock."

"And that's another thing," Caleb pointed out. "What would our parents say if I brought home a cocktail waitress from a strip club?"

"They'd probably say something like 'Thank God, he's finally getting laid'."

"And what would they say when they saw that she's out to here pregnant?" Caleb held his arms in a circle far from his stomach.

"They'd say…is it yours?" Connor started ticking off a count on his fingers.

"Stop it," Caleb yelled. "It can't be mine. I don't want a baby."

"Please, don't tell me you told her that. Please tell me you're not that stupid."

"It's not mine, okay? It can't be mine."

"I hope you're right…but I also kind of hope you're wrong."

Chapter Eight

"You're back!" Leah jumped from her bunk feeling that new sense of tightening around her extended abdomen and lowered herself back to her bunk. "Are you all right?"

"Well for pity sake, Tinkerbelle, anyone else would think you missed me." Rosie plopped down next to Leah on the lower bunk—something she'd never done before. "Do you know what segregation means to me in this hellhole? It means solitude, quiet reflection, the total lack of bullshit. I enjoyed it."

"I was afraid you'd be there longer."

"Big brother seemed to be working to my advantage this time." Rosie leaned against the back wall putting one foot onto the bed rail and resting the other over her raised knee. "Sign in sheets and surveillance cameras proved I couldn't have taken the shit under your mattress. Considering you're still here, I guess they cleared you too."

"Why did you take the blame?"

"It wouldn't have mattered for me. I'll be stuck in a cage for the rest of my life. You'll be out soon and have your whole life ahead of you. If you want to repay me, you'll keep your ass out of jail from now on. You're too nice to be in with these bitches and you have that baby to think of."

People here threw Leah's pregnancy in her face all

the time, but no one ever expressed concern for the baby. Hell, no one even referred to the baby at all. Leah swallowed the lump that had formed in her throat.

"You really are in a lot of trouble, aren't you, Rosie? If there's anything I could do to help…"

"I killed a man, Tinkerbelle, killed him deader than a roach in a puddle of Raid, and I'm not sorry. I had my reasons, but that's my own business. If you tell anybody, I'll hoist your pregnant ass up on the top bunk and leave you there for a week." After a few minute's pause, Rosie added, "There is one thing you could do for me." She stood and slid her bible out from under her pillow. Inside was an envelope. She removed a letter and picture, and handed the envelope to Leah. She held up the picture of a sweet, young teenage girl. "This is my baby, Yvonne, fourteen-years-old. She's staying with my mother at that return address. I don't allow her to come here, but she writes every week. I'd appreciate it if your lawyer friend would check on her for me. Maybe you could even look in on her when you get out. You take the envelope, but I'd like to keep the rest."

"Of course I will. Oh my God, she's so beautiful."

"Maybe a little too beautiful," Rosie mumbled with a frown. "I'm going to write her a letter before lunch."

"I think I'll go down to the common area. It's closer to the dining hall. It's easier to take these walks in a few shorter distances lately." Leah slid the envelope into the back pocket of her pants and stretched the kinks out of her back.

"Dining hall, ha. You make this place sound like a sorority house. You know," Rosie grinned, "I'll sit with my usual crowd and pretend like I don't know you."

"I wouldn't expect anything more."

Leah passed a number of cells where women were straightening their bunks and brushing their hair, in preparation for lunch. It was quiet like this before every meal. Even though it was a daily routine and the food wasn't great, meals were the biggest social events of the day. Unlike the exercise yard, you could sit indoors and relax with a small group. There was less need to watch your back when everyone carried a full tray.

The tightening in her belly had reached her back. Leah settled into the nearest chair in the common area to catch her breath. She'd realized in the last couple of days that the baby wasn't kicking as much. Was it getting so big it didn't have room to move? She felt as though the baby would be as big as she was by the time it arrived. Her next doctor appointment was a few days away. Now that she knew Rosie was a mother, maybe she'd talk to her about these new sensations. Yes, she'd make a point of it tonight before the lights went out.

Suddenly she heard high-pitched, muffled voices. Even though she couldn't tell what was being said, the voices sounded angry. The guards' office had a large window in the door. Through it, she saw three uniformed women. The one that concerned her most was Katya. She appeared to be tossing items from a desk drawer into a box. Throwing out a few final, indecipherable words, Katya headed for the door. Leah felt as though she was in the path of a hurricane with no time to find shelter.

"This is your fault! You are ruining everything for me!" Katya's voice was raw. She dropped the box and charged Leah like a rabid animal. "Tell me where the fucking money is!"

Before she could blink, Katya had a fist full of hair.

Leah flew off the back of the table and slid several feet on the tile floor. Landing on her right side, a huge pressure banded around her belly and water gushed between her legs.

An alarm, flashing lights, the clanging of cell doors all locking at once.

The two other guards and a few inmates who'd been outside of their cells ran toward her. They were all shouting but their voices seemed tinny and far away. A loud crack sounded from above. Katya fell beside her, facedown and unconscious. Another guard stood in the place she'd been with a nightstick in her raised hand.

***

Caleb pushed through the main doors of the hospital taking long purposeful strides. As soon as the front desk was in view he spoke without slowing.

"Maternity."

"Second floor, and then turn to the right," a volunteer behind the desk stated with one finger raised.

He stabbed the Up arrow by the elevator door three times before it slid open. Leah's cellmate had talked a guard into calling him. Between his office and the hospital parking lot she'd informed him about what had taken place in the jail's common area. Heads would roll. Just the day before, he'd warned the jail officials that Lebedev was a danger to Leah. She never should have been allowed to get so close to her. The woman was a monster and now they had proof, but at what cost?

A white-coated doctor stood outside a room whispering instructions to two nurses wearing pale green scrubs. Before he reached them, the nurses rushed away in different directions.

"Leah Fletcher."

"Come with me," the doctor replied.

Instead of taking him into a treatment room, the doctor led him to a private conference room and shut the door. He didn't offer Caleb a seat, nor did he take one. His body vibrated with a sense of urgency.

"My name is Doctor Bryan Falstaff. I'm the Chief of Obstetrics and just happened to be on call when Leannette was brought in. She's in pretty bad shape, which puts us in a precarious situation. Leannette, or Leah, took a hard hit to her back and head. It could cause complications in the delivery."

"Can you stop the labor?" Caleb asked. "I've heard of people doing that when the baby tries to come too early. It would give you a chance to check her out and make sure she's safe."

"It's too late for that."

"Then put her to sleep and take the baby by C-section."

"Let me explain." The doctor rubbed his hands over his face in frustration. "I don't mean to be callous, but her water broke with such force it more or less sucked the baby right down into the birth canal."

"What's the worst case scenario?" Caleb didn't want to think about it, didn't want to know, but it was time to man-up.

"There could be swelling or even bleeding in the brain. Also, she could have spinal damage. Pushing out a baby takes a lot of effort. I can't guarantee the outcome for the mother. If anything happens to her before we can get the baby out, it could also be in danger." The doctor wiped at his perspiring forehead with his shirtsleeve. "We don't have any options. The baby is coming."

The room swayed. Caleb grabbed the back of a chair. His mind slipped back six years. He pictured his bloody legs trapped under the steering column of his wrecked car, yards away from Brenda as she lay on wet pavement having her belly cut open by paramedics. There was nothing he could do but scream curses at God and the men around her. He wouldn't do that this time. Come hell or high water, he'd be beside Leah to hold her hand. He'd suffer the consequences along with her, whatever they may be.

"I understand." He took a deep breath to slow his racing heart. "I want to be there, but I won't get in your way."

"We'd all understand if you'd rather wait outside."

"No, I want to be there."

"I have my best labor and delivery nurse with her while we clean up and change. The baby is developed enough to be born under normal circumstances, but due to her condition, I have a neo-natal team standing by." He placed his hand on Caleb's shoulder. "We'll do all we can for them."

Chapter Nine

Leah felt like she'd been run over by a steamroller. Her arms and legs were the only parts of her body that weren't wracked with pain. The ambulance and emergency room attendants were more worried about moving quickly than seeing to her comfort. That was okay. The baby had to be taken care of first.

She'd never been around kids or people who had them. She hadn't been able to take birthing classes. Could she keep her wits about her enough to remember what she'd read from the two ragged, old books she'd found in the jail's minuscule library? Her head hurt so badly she could barely move it. It didn't matter that the pain in her back took her breath away. When another contraction hit, she curled into a tight ball.

Why had all this happened? What kind of way was this to bring a tiny baby into the world? Was the baby okay? Had it been injured in Katya's attack? She'd only cared about the money, money that, as far as Leah was concerned, didn't exist.

"Okay honey, when the next contraction starts I want you to concentrate on your focus point and control your breathing."

Leah looked up to find an extremely large man coming through the door. He had skin the color of milk chocolate and dreadlocks that hung past his shoulders tied behind his neck. He had a smile as big as the grill of a bus and soft, kind eyes.

"We want to even out that blood flow."

"I don't know what to do," she said. "I didn't get to take any classes."

"I was afraid of that." He motioned his thumb toward the door. "I saw Gretchen the evil guard outside."

"Oh my God," Leah moaned. "They're even watching me here?"

"Don't worry, sweetie. They won't come inside unless you threaten us or try to make a run for the door. You're one of the lucky ones. They sometimes have our patients cuffed to the bed rails. That won't happen today. For now, let's just worry about having a healthy baby. I'm going to help you through this. Let's call it on-the-job-training."

"Are you the doctor?"

"Oh no, darlin'," His deep baritone laugh made her smile. "My name is Marcus Lange. I'm the head nurse in this department. When the paperwork comes through, I'll be a full-fledged midwife. I've delivered more babies than sequins on a transvestite at Mardi Gras.

"Because of your injuries, Dr. Falstaff will be attending this birth. I saw him speaking to your partner as they were going to the locker room."

Marcus helped her learn to breathe through the next contraction.

"I don't have a partner."

"It seems you do. He's a tall, blond guy with muscles. If he isn't your partner, what is he?"

"He's my lawyer."

"Well, you must have given him a damned good

retainer because he's on the way." Marcus tapped her belly. "He appears to be devoted to you and this little hitchhiker."

Another contraction hit faster and stronger than the last few. Did Caleb suspect the truth? Was that why he seemed devoted? She stared into Marcus's eyes and mimicked the way he breathed. His method did seem to help.

"If you don't want him here, I can let him know. Just keep in mind I'll be taking my life in my hands." Marcus studied a strip of paper coming from a machine at her side. "Either way, this baby needs to be born soon. She's had a lot of excitement and she's a tired little girl."

"I don't know if it's a girl or a boy."

"She's a girl all right. I guess every baby's sex before it's born and my success rate is in the high nineties. I'd bet my life on this little one being a female."

Per Marcus's instructions, Leah forced herself to lay flat and concentrate on her fingers and toes. It only took a minute before her hands and feet were limp. The steady breathing also made her back and head pain more manageable. When the next contraction came she stared into Marcus's eyes. After each long inhale through her nose she exhaled three short pants through her mouth. It was miraculous how much easier the episode passed.

The door to Leah's left flew open and Caleb swooped to her side in a single step. His hair stood on end and his eyes were so wide she feared they'd pop out of their sockets. His complexion was as pale as his green scrubs that matched the nurses. He grabbed her hand.

"Are you all right?"

"I think so," Leah replied. "Do I look as bad as you?"

"You look more beautiful than I've ever seen you."

"Take a deep breath while I check you," the doctor said from the foot of the bed. He lifted the sheet a few inches to slide his arm between her legs. Two gloved fingers pushed into a place that no one had accessed in a while. "The baby is moving along. It's almost time to push."

The strongest contraction so far slammed into her. Leah looked to Marcus, inhaling deeper, panting loudly and more forcefully. When she could speak again, she did so with gusto. "Holy, fucking hell!"

"Is that normal?" Caleb asked the doctor. "She doesn't usually use that kind of language."

The doctor's laugh was cut short by a commotion outside the door. When it flew open Marcus filled the space with his large body. "The waiting room is down the hall, folks. We're not selling tickets."

The first person Leah saw was Petrov, the Russian. "I beg your pardon, sir, but I've come for my grandchild."

Then Leah saw her mother, completely inebriated, swing from Petrov's sleeve nearly landing against Marcus's wide chest. "I'm going to name him Little Bogdan, sweetie," she slurred then turned glassy eyes to her husband. "We can raise him as if he was our own."

"What is he doing here?" Petrov pointed at Caleb. "That man has no right to be here. I don't want him near the child."

"Look mister, I don't know who you are and I

don't care," Marcus blurted. "If you don't get away from this door we'll have you removed by armed guards. No one crosses this threshold."

"Just a minute," another voice interrupted. The social worker who'd visited Leah once in jail stepped forward with two correctional officers at her back. "Who is that man? My paperwork doesn't show a husband or domestic partner. No father has been named. How did he get in there?"

"I need to push!" Leah bellowed.

"You can figure that out after our work is done!" Marcus shouted. "We have a mother and child in distress here and if anyone interrupts again I'll take them apart with my bare hands." He forced the door shut and flipped the lock.

****

"If I don't get through this, you have to protect the baby." Leah grabbed the front of Caleb's shirt and pulled him closer. "Name her Isabelle, after my grandma. I'd like to call her Belle."

"We'll both protect her," Caleb replied. "Everything is going to be all right."

Panic prickled every nerve in Caleb's body when Leah's second screaming push brought her tiny baby girl into the world. He watched as the child was handed to a young female nurse. She was a bundle of arms, legs and a patch of black curls. Leah though, was limp and lifeless.

"No!"

He held her hand and kissed her once on the cheek before she was whisked away. There was so much he wished he'd had time to say to her. They'd just witnessed a miracle, and now he didn't know if she'd ever have the chance to hold her baby. If she did live, she could be in a coma or severally brain damaged. What about her back injury. Would she ever walk again? Had that miracle been worth all she may have sacrificed for it?

A sound like the squall of a kitten came from a huddle of nurses. Little Belle wore a pink knitted cap and striped blanket. She appeared to be trying to kick her way out of her tightly wrapped cocoon. One nurse slid a card into an opening at the end of her glass bassinette. Baby Girl Fletcher, weight 5 lb. 2 oz., length 18 inches.

"Belle."

The three nurses turned curious faces to him.

"Make sure they know her name is Belle…Isabelle."

Caleb passed the nurse's station on his way to the elevator. He was stopped by the male nurse, Marcus. "I'm telling you, this is the baby's father," he insisted to the social worker. "You've got no right to take her away.

Trust me, I won't let those horrible people near her. We'll find a suitable home to place the child until a judge decides what will happen next."

"You can't just take the baby to strangers," Caleb argued. "She's too small, she needs care."

"The baby has been deemed perfectly healthy, sir. As long as she's over five pounds, she can be removed from the hospital." The woman crossed her arms and raised a brow. "May I ask who you are and how you're related?"

"My name is Caleb McCrae. I'm a bar certified attorney specializing in family law." He took a deep breath for courage. "I'm the father of Leah Fletcher's baby."

"You see?" Marcus berated her. "This is why he was called to the hospital. I don't know how you could not know this. It's on the record."

Caleb knew Marcus was lying, but he was just as desperate for the woman to believe him. If they lost possession of Belle, Petrov would have the perfect opportunity to move in.

"Oh," the poor woman murmured. "My paperwork doesn't seem to be complete. I'll just need a little more information from you, Mr. McCrae. Then you can take your daughter home."

"I'll get all her things together for you while you do that." Marcus winked. "We'll make sure you have everything you need for the first few days."

Marcus's encouragement didn't do a thing to lessen the stark terror screaming through Caleb's mind. What had he just done?

Chapter Ten

Caleb had only been home for two hours. The baby had slept most of that time, but now she was screaming like a pint-sized banshee. The pounding on his sitting room door added to the chaos. Pulling every strand of hair out of his head wouldn't make it feel any worse.

"Just a minute," he yelled as he stomped out of his bedroom.

Marcus had watched the baby for several hours that evening while Caleb sat in the emergency room waiting for news of Leah. Finally he'd had to go home for some sleep so he'd brought Belle to Caleb in a car seat, courtesy of the hospital. He'd also supplied him with a bag of diapers, a case of premade bottles, and a few gowns and blankets from the nursery. Who knew babies required so much stuff?

Marcus explained what a hard job babies had being born and that she'd mostly sleep for the first few days. That was only a few hours ago. So, what gave her the energy to scream the paint off the walls?

He threw the door open when another round of pounding started. In the hallway were his parents and Miss Hannah, all in their nightclothes. Okay, he wasn't at his best, but falling back a step with a collective gasp seemed a little dramatic.

"My God, you look like death warmed over," his father stated.

"What is all that caterwauling?" Miss Hannah and his mother pushed past him and headed for the bedroom.

"You may as well join the party."

"Don't mind if I do." Ian eyed him with a raised brow as they followed the women.

Caleb knew he should be embarrassed by the stacks of socks and underwear on the top of his dresser, but he'd had to think of some place to put the baby. The towels he'd lined the dresser drawer with were the softest things he could think of. He couldn't leave her scrunched up in the car seat.

"This poor baby is soaked through," Miss Hannah groused.

"Has this formula been warmed?" Melly picked up the tiny half-full bottle by his alarm clock.

"It must be warm. She threw it up as soon as she drank it. I'd throw up warm milk too," Caleb defended. "I've got diapers here somewhere."

"Did you burp her?"

"What?"

Ian cleared his throat loudly, drawing everyone's attention.

"I think the more important question is…where the hell did this baby come from?"

"She belongs to a client. It's a custody case."

"Don't you think you may have stepped over the line a little, son?" Ian asked.

"Ian," Melly interrupted. "This baby can't be more than a few hours old."

"Mom, Dad, I can explain everything."

"And you've got a lot of explaining to do." Miss Hannah held the baby against her chest exposing her naked bottom to the group.

"The birth mark," Melly cried.

Just above the crack between her tiny round cheeks was a diamond shaped red patch. There was a moment of silence before Belle released a resounding burp.

"She's a McCrae," Ian declared.

"It's just a little gas, Dad."

"The birth mark, you idiot." Ian smacked the back of Caleb's head. "Me, you, your brother, even little Cole has the same mark."

There was no denying his daughter any longer. In his heart, he'd known from the first day he'd seen Leah in the jail. Why hadn't she just admitted it when he asked? Then he remembered. She'd been afraid of losing custody of the baby. No matter what the future had in store for them, he'd never do that to her.

While Miss Hannah tended to the baby, Caleb took his parents to the sitting room and spilled the whole story: his history with Leah, her incarceration, the Russian and his associate who had caused Belle's sudden arrival. They all agreed her case was more than likely connected to Ted's attack in the parking garage.

"I want every scrap of paper you and Ted have put together on this case. We have people who can cover everything else in the office," Ian said. "This is family. All our efforts go to Leah until she's home with my granddaughter safe and sound. I'll call Connor back from down south if I have to."

"I can handle this, Dad."

"You have more important things to worry about," Melly said. "Miss Hannah and I will look after the baby while you get some sleep. You'll want to return to the hospital first thing in the morning and see about Leah."

"And for heaven sake, son," Ian added, "take a shower and shave first. It's no wonder that poor baby was screaming."

****

Petrov straightened the cuffs of his charcoal suit as he walked down the steps of the courthouse. He wasn't concerned whether or not Katya was keeping up with him. He didn't like being in the position of posting bail. He should have waited for his attorney to arrive.

"They put me in segregation—as though I'm afraid of being with the others. Not one of them frightens me. They all know I'm superior in strength as well as intelligence."

"So superior you'd attack a pregnant woman…unprovoked…in front of witnesses." He smirked. When his black Mercedes sedan pulled to the curb, Petrov climbed into the backseat, leaving his cousin to follow.

"This has gone on long enough, Bogdan." Katya's makeup was smudged. She reminded him of his wife. He checked his own appearance in the rearview mirror and exchanged a knowing glance with his driver, Ivan, as she rambled. "We should have that money and be resting on the beach in Miami by now."

"Miami is for old ladies who play bridge."

"I don't care where we go," Katya cried. "You've let her get away with too much. You should punish her until she gives you that money. Why not turn *her* over to those friends of yours?"

"You've done enough damage," Petrov said. "The baby came yesterday. Leah was too weak and injured. She's in a critical state. If she doesn't survive, this has all been for nothing, my marriage to that drunken sot, working a menial job, building contacts, arranging Leah's arrest, everything. The money will be lost."

"But, you have the baby now…right?"

"No! I do not have the baby. Even if I did, what good would that do? You are more stupid than I ever imagined."

Katya pouted for a short moment before trying a different tactic. "I don't have to be here for this stupid hearing. The judge will surely rule against me. We should leave the state. We can go anywhere. You don't need that money. You can make twice as much anywhere. You've done it before."

"Don't worry, Katya my love, I wouldn't think of making you stay for the hearing. I agree it wouldn't go well for you." The car turned a corner bringing her apartment house into view. Petrov tingled with anticipation. "Let's go inside and discuss your future."

As soon as the car was parked by the curb, Ivan was at Katya's door to help her step out. She turned to Petrov with a suspicious expression.

"No need for alarm, my little kitten," he laughed. "Ivan will be leaving with me. Your last punishment was obviously not effective. There's no need to repeat it." Petrov led her down the hallway to her apartment. His driver followed. He opened her door with his own key. "Instead, I have a surprise for you." Petrov smiled.

Katya found her full suitcases lined up along the entry. "Oh, Bogdan, we are leaving. This is wonderful. Where are we going now?" She checked the coat closet. "It'll be just like old times. We'll be back on top before you know it."

"I won't be going anywhere, dear cousin. My mission here is going to take longer than I'd planned.

Getting my money back from the Fletcher girl has become complicated."

"Anywhere I go won't be as much fun without you." She pouted again. "We can work together and make twice what Fletcher stole from you. You don't need her. She's caused nothing but trouble."

"I don't see it that way." Petrov dropped into her chair. "You've never understood that it's not about money, it's about taking back what is mine, taking back my pride. My plan was moving along nicely until you ruined everything. I don't know why I spent so much money getting you back from the L'vov Logovo."

"Don't say that, darling. I'll go anywhere you like. I'll do whatever you want."

"Yes. You'll go…but it won't be me giving you orders any more."

The bedroom door opened revealing a tall, muscular man with pale skin and short platinum hair. A scar trailing down his right brow, bisected the surface of his eye, blinding it and changing it from icy blue to cloudy white. It was her former boss, Adrik Sokolov, The Ghost. He had come to take her back to his club, back to Moscow. Petrov wanted to laugh at Katya's shocked expression.

"You'll be glad to know I was able to get back all the money I'd paid for you, plus a little profit. You must be a much better slave than you are a correctional officer." Petrov stood and walked to the door. "Well, as they say, if the handcuffs fit…"

As he strode to the exit he could still hear his cousin begging him to let her stay. He loved to make people beg, but it never changed his mind. In the backseat of the car he lit a celebratory cigar.

Chapter Eleven

Every cell in Leah's body screamed in pain. Someone was using her head as a conga drum. She was afraid to open her eyes for fear they'd explode. No part of her body seemed normal. She wished the voices around her would be quiet so she could go back to sleep. Everything had been okay until she'd woken.

Something strange about the voices tugged at her attention. They were male. For as long as she'd been in jail, the morning shift guards had all been female. Had something happened to bring the front office people to the women's area? They couldn't have replaced all the guards over night. Why wasn't Rosie humming? She always hummed church hymns while they prepared for the day. It was morning, wasn't it? What time was it?

"There's not much more we can do but wait for the swelling to go down," one man said. "It shouldn't get any worse, but we'll keep an eye on her."

"I didn't expect her face to be so puffy and bruised." It was Cal. What was he doing here? "Will there be any long term effects?"

"We relieved as much pressure as we could. We won't know any more until she wakes. She's not in a coma, but we don't know how she'll react to the anesthesia we had to give her. It could be minutes or hours." The strange voice must be a medical doctor. Was he talking about her? She wanted to tell them she was awake, but her throat was so dry it felt raw. Why were they here? Was something wrong with the baby?

Leah slowly placed her hands over her middle, but all she found beneath them was her own sore, swollen belly. The firm ball holding her child was gone. A long painful cry tore its way out of her chest and through her throat. They'd taken her baby.

"No, no, no," Caleb crooned. He held a straw to her lips. "Don't try to talk until you've had a little water. Everything's okay. You're going to be just fine, sweetheart."

Warm breath touched her cheek and she could smell Caleb's spicy cologne. How dare he take her baby, or had something bad happened to it? Why was he calling her sweetheart, was she dying? She swept her hand out, felt it connect with plastic, and heard a splash on a bare floor.

"My baby," she groaned.

"She's fine. Marcus took her down to the pediatric wing to be checked. He'll have her back in a few minutes." Caleb touched her cheek. "Open your eyes for me, honey. The doctor is waiting to look you over."

Leah slowly opened her eyes and blinked a few times. Nothing. The room was as dark as when they'd been closed.

"Don't turn the lights on," she said. "My head hurts too much. Who is Marcus?"

"Leah, can you tell me how many fingers I'm holding up."

"Of course not." She turned her head toward the second voice. "It's as dark as pitch in here. Can't we do this test some other time? I'd like a dim light to see my baby when she gets here. I take it she's a girl. Why did you take her early? And why can't I remember? Who is Marcus?"

"Marcus is the best and most trusted nurse on my staff. He helped with the delivery," the doctor said. "What is the last thing you remember?"

"I was talking to Rosie on my bunk." She turned in the direction Caleb's voice had been. "It's very important that I tell you about our conversation."

"We'll have plenty of time for that soon." Caleb took her hand in his. "What happened after you spoke to Rosie?"

"Nothing…at least I don't remember anything." Leah gripped the blanket in her free hand. "It's so strange. Did I pass out? What time is it? It must be the middle of the night, unless there's been a power failure. Don't hospitals usually have backup systems?"

"Leah," Caleb said softly. "The last time you saw Rosie was yesterday, around noon. That was twenty-two hours ago."

"Nonsense." Leah jerked her hand away. "Turn the light on and bring me my baby. I want my baby."

"Just relax and listen to me, Leah." The doctor laid his hand on her shoulder. "The lights are on. The curtains are open. Your vision seems to be impaired, but I'm fairly certain it's a temporary condition. We'll have a specialist here very soon."

"No. No, that can't be right. I can't be blind. I have responsibilities." Leah struggled against the doctor's grip on her shoulder. Caleb held her down from the other side. Panic built in her chest causing her heart to race. "I have to go. I have to find my baby."

Suddenly Caleb's arms were around her shoulders. His hip was against her leg. "Leah, honey, don't struggle and don't get too loud. There's a guard outside the door. She'll handcuff you to the bed if you try to leave the room."

Leah heard the door open. She froze.

"Our little Belle is the most perfect baby the pediatrician has ever seen. He didn't say those exact words, but I could tell he envied me her company." The voice was deep and ethnic in tone. "She's been chewing my finger off though. Is her momma ready to feed her?"

"We have a problem." The doctor explained the situation and asked Marcus to stay with Leah while he made a few phone calls.

"Marcus will take care of you and Belle," Caleb promised. "Believe me, no one is more capable. I'll be back in a few minutes."

****

Caleb followed the doctor into the hallway. He waited for the door to close, cutting off their conversation from Leah.

"What the hell is going on? You didn't tell me she'd be blind."

"I believe it's an unforeseen side effect of the hydrocephalus. That's the condition that caused her brain to swell." The doctor motioned him further from the door. "The pressure of pushing the baby out is what caused her to pass out. My guess is it affected her optical nerves. It can have the same result as a tight rubber band around your finger. Only a specialist can say for sure. Hopefully, her sight will return once the swelling goes down. It's not unusual to have lost a bit of memory. That may even be a blessing, considering the circumstances."

"She can't go back to jail if she can't see to defend herself."

The doctor shook his head. "After the way she was beaten, I'm going to keep her here as long as I can. Something else is bothering me though."

"What's that?"

"I'd like someone to be with her as much as possible and help her care for the baby. I think it would do wonders for her state of mind. The problem is, she'll have to return to jail eventually…alone. That'll be the toughest thing she's ever faced. It could set back her recovery or even prevent it."

After the doctor walked away to make his calls, Caleb stepped back inside Leah's room. He found Marcus sitting in a chair next to her bed as she fed Belle from her breast. His breath hitched. Her smiling face was aglow with joy and contentment. Taking custody of that baby would be the cruelest thing he could imagine.

Belle's blanket had been removed to allow Leah's fingers to check every tiny digit on her hands and feet. She felt the wispy curls on her head and the chubby cheeks as they worked to extract her milk.

Suddenly Caleb seemed lonely, separated from the world. He felt like a street urchin peeking inside a family's window on Christmas morning.

"Cal, is that you?" Leah asked.

"I should do my rounds while your family gets to know each other." Marcus stood. "You share a beautiful baby. I must say, she's my masterpiece."

Caleb took the chair Marcus had vacated. He didn't know what to say.

"Tell me what she looks like, Cal."

"Oh, let's see." He cleared his throat, but the knot

that had formed there was too stubborn to swallow. "She has curly black hair, like you. Her skin is still a little red, but I'm told that'll change. As you can tell, it's as soft as yours. Her eyes are big and round—again, like yours. However, they're blue like mine and I'm also told they're a shade that will stay blue. Her cheeks are fat, but I think it's because she doesn't have any teeth."

"That's something I'm grateful for at the moment," Leah laughed. "What else?"

"She has the ugliest thing I've ever seen attached to her belly button and when she takes a notion to scream, she turns a bright shade of purple."

"Tell me more," Leah said.

"Well, last but certainly not least, she has a tiny round bum with my family's birthmark right at the top."

Leah's smile fell. The hand she'd been using to feel her baby's digits wrapped around Belle's body securely.

"You should have told me." Caleb placed his hand over hers. "How could you think I'd separate a good mother from her baby? I go to court all the time with people tearing each other to pieces using their children as weapons. I see the confusion, turmoil, and absolute fear in those children's eyes. The decision about a child's future should never be made by who has the most money or power."

"But what if the parents can't get along?" she asked. "What if their lives are too different?"

"The key is cooperation. You and Belle will have everything I can afford to provide, and that's quite a lot."

When Leah frowned, Caleb tried to figure out what

he said wrong. He didn't have to wonder long.

"I've taken care of myself for a long time. I think I can take care of one small child. That is…if…"

"Your sight will return. Don't allow yourself to believe otherwise." The baby had fallen asleep and Leah covered herself, looking embarrassed. Caleb wished they knew each other well enough to share the experience without awkwardness. Thank heaven she couldn't see him staring.

Her nipples were much darker than he remembered. He recalled how they felt and how they'd reacted to his touch. He recalled every detail of that night like he did every night when he closed his eyes. His fingers ached to touch her hair. He wanted to put his arms around her and put her head on his shoulder. Why hadn't he looked for her sooner, harder? The answer was easy. He didn't feel he deserved her.

They'd only had one night together and it had mostly been spent having sex—fabulous, mind-blowing sex. But, he'd done the same with a few women and never had them haunt his dreams the way Leah had. His attraction to her had been more than physical. They'd shared a crossword puzzle, cold pizza, and comfortable silence. That was rare in his world, especially after he'd driven the woman home in a bright new BMW sports car. Leah hadn't cared about his money then and now she acted like he was forcing it on her.

"You'll have a new job when you come home. You're a mother now. That'll take every minute of your time."

"That sounds good, but not very realistic. I will always have bills to pay." A smile crossed her lips so briefly he wasn't sure he'd seen one at all. "What about now? You're too busy to care for a baby and I doubt you have much experience."

"That's true," he said. "But I have Miss Hannah. She was our nanny and now she keeps house for my parents. Well, to be honest, she runs the house. She can't keep her hands off this little one."

"Your family has seen her? They'll surely encourage you to take custody of her."

"That's not true. They believe in family and expect me to do what is best for you and Belle both. As a matter of fact, my father is helping me work on having your case reviewed. I don't want to get your hopes too high, but I think we're close. As soon as Miss Hannah gets here to look after the two of you, I have an appointment to meet my father in the judge's chambers."

"Why would the judge change his mind now? It would be admitting he was wrong."

"He was wrong, I can prove it." Caleb pushed a curl back from her forehead. "Besides, we're meeting with a different judge, one higher up on the food chain."

Belle stretched in Leah's arms and then curled back into a restful sleep.

"I love the name Belle. What made you decide to call her that?"

"You told me to, just before she was born. You wanted to name her after your grandmother." Caleb chuckled. "I'm glad you approve. I made out her birth certificate this morning. Her name is Isabelle Rose McCrae. I hope you don't mind that I gave her Rosie's name, too. We owe her at least that much."

A cloud passed over Leah's expression. He'd

expected his decision to give Belle his last name would conjure a lively discussion. Instead she changed the subject. "I'm glad you realize how much Rosie has helped. I think she needs us as well."

While they waited for Miss Hannah, Leah filled him in on her last conversation with her cellmate. Thankfully, Caleb found the envelope with Rosie's address in Leah's property bag.

Chapter Twelve

Ian McCrae had a lot of clout in the city of Tampa and Hillsborough County, but Caleb still couldn't help being impressed. His father had reviewed Leah's case overnight, coming to the same conclusions as he and Ted. The whole thing seemed like a setup.

At one in the afternoon he was being shown into Judge Banyan's office. Waiting with Ian and the judge was the county prosecutor, Randall Lowry.

"The evidence was overwhelming," Lowry declared. "She was given a minor sentence considering she'd never been in trouble before. I don't see any reason to reopen the case or reverse the decision."

"Hell, I'm not talking about a mistrial, Randall. This case never should have happened," Ian shouted. "The problem isn't about what's in the reports. I'm concerned with what is missing."

"Go on, Ian," Judge Banyan said.

"An anonymous caller reported that he knew where the stolen merchandise was, but no one seems to have asked how he came onto this information. There was no attempt to identify the man. How do we know he wasn't the one that placed the items where they were found? For all we know, he could have been the robber.

"Miss Fletcher wasn't interviewed, but instead her door was practically knocked off its hinges in a raid— an illegal raid, in my opinion. I'm surprised they didn't have a SWAT team standing by. After all, Miss Fletcher is all of five-feet-two and a hundred pounds. The items were found in seconds because the caller told them exactly where to look. They were under a sofa that was twice Miss Fletcher's weight. Miss Fletcher had been home less than an hour. She'd been at work during the robbery. However, her work records hadn't been checked. Her manager and co-workers were never spoken to." He paused for a breath.

"She was born and raised in that house. Everyone in the neighborhood knew her. No one we've spoken to had seen a guest in her home in months. And, believe me, they keep an eye on the place. Her mother's drunken antics are legendary. What's more, not one person on her block has been questioned by the police. Not by anyone…before my own investigator canvassed the area a few days ago. The only witness at her hearing was a detective, Horace Weinstein, who has a long record of breaking rules and receiving disciplinary actions. He's been suspected of being on the take, but everyone's too close-mouthed to admit it. He's a department joke. According to his notes, the only person he talked to was her mother who stumbled into him in the driveway. She was inebriated as usual and didn't have any information. Hell, she could hardly remember her own name. Now you tell me, your Honor, would you have seen this case the same way? Would you have signed that search warrant?"

"Not from what you've told me. I suppose you know Judge Zeigler is out of the country. I don't want to give him time to come back and throw a wrench into the works. I intend to have this straightened out by the end of the week." He frowned at the prosecutor who was reading the packet of information Ian had provided. Then, he pushed a button on his desk phone. "Gladys, I want Sheriff Burns in my office, along with Detective Horace Weinstein, as soon as possible."

"Your Honor," Caleb interrupted. "There's another complication."

"I heard about the baby. Congratulations. Your father bragged my ear off until Randall arrived. Surely a little thing like her can't be that much trouble. Ian said you have help taking care of her."

"Yes, sir. The problem is Leah. Her injuries have caused what we hope is temporary blindness. The doctor is keeping her at the hospital as long as he can, but she's on the county's dime. We can't let her go back to the jail in her condition. I'm afraid to think what another attack might do to her and she wouldn't be able to defend herself."

"My God," Ian mumbled.

"I'm sorry to hear that," Lowry added.

"You should be," Ian snapped. "She shouldn't have been there in the first place."

Judge Banyan slammed a paperweight on his desktop to get their attention. "I'm releasing Miss Fletcher into your custody, Caleb. You'll be responsible for seeing that she doesn't leave town until this matter is cleared up. Also, you'll be responsible for her safety. Take her to your parents' house and let her spend time with her baby. That place is a fortress. Would that be satisfactory?"

"Yes, sir." Caleb shook his hand. "That would be more than satisfactory."

****

"Mr. Petrov, we don't allow smoking inside the

shop." The hairdresser pinched her nose as though his twenty-dollar cigar smelled worse than the black dye on his hair.

"I paid a lot of money to come here after normal hours. Do you know why?" Petrov watched her head shake. "I like this shop. It's clean and classy. I may decide to come here regularly. I won't be able to do that if it's no longer standing. Do you get my meaning?"

"Yes." The girl handed him an empty mixing dish for his ashes. A loud rap on the glass door sent her scurrying to the front entry. A moment later she returned. "A man with a gold badge says he needs to talk to you. I had to let him in."

Petrov suddenly regretted having his driver, Ivan, wait in the back parking lot.

Weinstein sauntered in and sat in the chair opposite him. "Well, look at you, all slicked up with that goop in your hair. I had a hell of a time tracking you down."

"How did you find me?" Petrov asked. "Having me watched could be very bad for your health, you know."

"Ha, I don't have the pull to order a tail for you. I know where those two goons of yours hang out. They told me it was time for your beauty treatment. I knew you'd pick a posh place like this. After all, I am the best detective this county's ever had."

"Why are you here, Weinstein?" Petrov made a mental note to reprimand George and Carl for their indiscretion.

"I love the way you say my name with that funny accent. Anyway, I seem to have a little problem. I've been suspended until they look into my investigation regarding the Fletcher girl. They feel the paperwork was, let's say, light, on the case. A different judge named Banyan is getting involved. He's got balls. He raked the sheriff and county prosecutor over the coals today. I told him I took my orders from Judge Zeigler, instead of the other way around. I don't figure that asshole will show his face around here for a while, anyway."

"Damn!" Petrov rolled his cigar between his lips as he thought a moment. "Do you know if they've sent the Fletcher girl back to jail?"

"Well, that's where the problem becomes yours, and it's a big one. From what I understand, the new judge has released her to that lawyer friend of hers. He'll no doubt take her to his parents' house. That place is huge. No telling how big the staff is there and the place is more secure than Fort Knox."

He'd lost the cop, the judge, and Katya because of their stupid, sloppy handling of the situation. Now, he wouldn't have access to the girl or the baby. All he had left was a drunken, clingy wife, her dilapidated old house, and a sleazy strip club job. He had to find a way to draw Leah to him.

"I'll call when I need you again."

"Anytime, man," Weinstein chuckled. "I could use the extra money while I'm out of work."

"I don't think you'll have to worry about that long."

While the hairdresser led the detective to the front of the salon, Petrov used his cell phone to call Ivan. "Weinstein is just leaving from the front. Intercept him and hold him until I'm finished. Use any method necessary."

Chapter Thirteen

Ted walked into Caleb's office.

"Who do you have watching Leah?" Caleb asked.

"A buddy of mine, Jake Scott, volunteered his time. He's a uniform cop who worked the raid on her apartment. He says this thing's been on his mind ever since. He knew from the get-go that something was wonky about it. He feels like he owes her. Don't worry. He has a spotless reputation and he's built like a linebacker. I have to admit, though, I'd be more afraid of getting through Miss Hannah. She took to Leah and the baby like they were her cubs."

"Is that Rosie's file?" Caleb eyed the thick folder in Ted's lap.

"Yeah, with a few of my own notes. Going into her neighborhood should earn me combat pay. There isn't a building that doesn't sport at least a dozen bullet holes. It's terrifying to think children are growing up in that place. What chance do the poor kids have?" Ted flipped through the pages as he continued.

"The transcripts are what I expected. Rosie, or Rosalie Washington, killed a gangbanger, Teno Jenkins, a.k.a. Easy-T, in an alley behind her building. I think he was pretty high up on the food chain. She didn't use a conventional weapon, just a two-by-four with a few rusty nails sticking out of it. It came from a pile of debris by a dumpster. It was broad daylight with no place to hide. No premeditation. Funny thing is, the banger had a gun in the pocket of his pants and never drew it. His pants were around his ankles. Had he pulled them down or did they fall down, we don't know. You know how these kids wear them halfway down their asses.

The bottom line is: Rosie refused to say why she did it. She hasn't defended herself at all."

"Did you talk to her mother?"

"Wouldn't let me in. She said Rosie told her not to speak to anyone. I peeked through the chain on the door. Clarice Washington doesn't look much older than Rosie. I think they must have both been teenage mothers. But, you can see the worry is wearing on her."

"I may know a way to get my foot in the door." Caleb thought for a minute. "Do you have anything else?"

"Do I ever come back empty handed?" Ted smirked. "An old lady in the next apartment was willing to talk to me. She practically dragged me inside. I can't say I minded though, she makes the best damned peanut butter cookies on the planet. She says Rosie was a good mother. She worked at the grocery store during the day and at the movie theater at night. She usually walked her daughter home from school between shifts, but that day she'd had to work a few minutes late. By the time she caught up to Yvonne, Easy-T had her cornered in the back alley. He'd been harassing the girl for weeks. The old lady didn't know any more than Yvonne was screaming and Rosie was standing over the body with the bloody two-by-four. She took the kid inside before the cops arrived. She and the grandma have been holed up there ever since. Miss Bonita, of the peanut butter cookies, figures they're getting by on Clarice's disability check, and food she and a few neighbors have been bringing them. They told her Yvonne is taking virtual school from her computer.

"She's worried. Easy-T's boys have been hanging around more than usual."

"I'll find a way to get them out of there. It's a dangerous situation for everyone living in the building."

"Shit, Cal, leaving for work in the morning is dangerous for those people." Ted gave an exaggerated shudder. "Is there anything else you'd like to know?"

"Yeah," Caleb rubbed at his eyes. "Can I ever expect to sleep again?"

"Believe me, man, it's a hell of a lot easier when you have a partner," Ted laughed. "You can take turns waking up in the night."

"Getting up is no problem. I never have a chance to lie down. That little Siren goes off all night long. The only time she's quiet is when she's eating. Do you think I should take her back to the doctor?"

"What does Leah think?"

"Belle's as quiet as a mouse when she's with Leah…or Miss Hannah…or my mom. Hell, she's great with anyone except me. She hates me!"

Ted patted Caleb's shoulder while he had a good chuckle. "Taking care of an infant is easier than it seems. Wait until she gets those little legs under her and her curiosity kicks into high gear. At this point all she needs is three things: a meal, a diaper, or a cuddle. You can handle that.

"By the way, Jenny wants to give Leah a shower as soon as she's feeling up to it."

"Why the hell would she want to do that?"

****

Leah didn't know if it was her hopeful imagination, but it seemed as though the moving figures in her vision were more pronounced. She'd stopped taking the pain meds after the first one in order to nurse the baby safely, but her headaches had greatly improved anyway. The only thing she wanted was to get well and be able to care for Belle on her own. Not to say that Miss Hannah wasn't wanted. She'd been a godsend. Leah had never felt so spoiled. But, sooner or later she had to get back to a normal life. Sooner sounded great, now that she knew she didn't have to go back to jail.

Thinking about jail made her recall Rosie's situation. She'd have to ask Cal how that was going. For now, she'd trust him and not let it ruin a nice day.

"Looks like we've got company," Miss Hannah said. "Mr. Caleb is coming down the hall with a nice sized box under his arm. I wonder if that present's for me."

Leah sat up straighter and fingered her curls into place.

"Now don't you worry, missy, you look as pretty as a porcelain doll."

"I feel more like a rag doll."

A moment later, spicy cologne wafted toward her and warm lips touched her forehead.

"I brought something for you to wear home," Caleb whispered. A light weight box was placed on her lap. "The doctor is releasing you today."

"Oh, so soon?" Her elation only lasted a few seconds. "I can't go home. The Russian is living in our house. He'd only be a few yards away from Belle. I can't protect her."

"You're coming home with me. My mother is getting a room ready for you as we speak."

"Does she have the space? I don't want to impose."

"Honey child," Miss Hannah laughed, "the McCraes have enough room for the hundred-and-first-airborne-division. Besides that, she'd add another wing to the house if you and Belle needed it. You won't be an imposition at all."

Leah fumbled with the box until she managed to remove the lid. "Tell me what it looks like."

"The blouse is loose and sleeveless in a kelly green silk," Miss Hannah said. "It goes with a stretchy broom skirt with tiny lines of every color you can imagine. There's a pair of black canvas pull-on shoes. We also have a nursing bra and red silk panties."

"Red silk!"

"Miss Hannah, I think you missed your calling." Caleb swept the box away. "You should be a speaker at those fashion shows."

"How did you know my sizes?" Leah exclaimed.

"I had Ted do a little recon from your apartment. His wife made the necessary adjustments and suggested the styles. I just asked her what she wished she could have worn when she came home from the hospital."

"Oh wow, that outfit sure beats the heck out of a handful of balloons." Leah tracked the sound of the nurse's voice as she entered and moved around the room. "I brought your release papers to sign. As soon as you're ready, we'll have a wheelchair standing by to take you downstairs." She pulled an envelope from her clipboard. "By the way, a lady dropped this by the nurse's station a few minutes ago."

While the nurse led her hand to the lines she had to

sign, Caleb tore open the envelope.

"What is it?" Leah asked when the nurse had left.

"A card from your mother."

A chill crept up her spine. "What does it say?"

"She just wishes you well."

"I know better than that. My mother doesn't play that game. Her world revolves around no one but herself. What does it really say?"

"It says, Dear L., I can't wait to have that baby in my arms. Bogdan will make such a wonderful grandpa. I hope you'll give us a chance and accept him as the man I love."

"It makes me sick to know she's married to the man who killed my father. She lives in her own little world and doesn't even realize who he is. What else does she say?"

"That's it."

"Cal, I'm depending on you. I need to be able to trust you more than you realize. I can tell by the tone of your voice that something more is bothering you. Please tell me what it is."

Leah heard Cal take a deep breath.

"There's a note from Petrov on the back. It says, *just remember, I still have leverage.*" The paper crinkled. Caleb added, "We should try to get her away from him."

"It's no use. She'd fight you every step of the way. She's had boyfriends who've badly abused her, but she defended them until the day they walked out on her. As long as Petrov buys her booze and shows her a little attention, he owns her."

Chapter Fourteen

"I wish we'd had this elevator back when I was twelve. I spent the entire summer in a leg cast limping up and down the stairs. I was miserable."

"You could have slid down the banister."

"That's how I broke my leg in the first place," Caleb said. "My father had it installed a few years ago as a surprise for Miss Hannah. She grumbled about not being too old to climb the stairs, but she still uses it every day."

Today it was big enough to carry him and a wheelchair for Leah with Belle in her lap. The gifts and flowers she'd received at the hospital would require a second trip.

"I appreciate the star treatment, Cal, but I think I could have managed a set of stairs with a little help."

"You have no idea where you are." Caleb laughed. "Your room is on the third floor, west wing, near my suite. The east wing holds my brother's rooms when his family visits. The central rooms are for casual entertainment, like the theater, arcade, and such. My parents use the second floor west wing. The east is all guest rooms; central rooms are for more formal entertainment, the biggest being the music room of course. On the ground floor we have the main parlor, Dad's den, formal dining room, and kitchen. At the east end is the indoor/outdoor pool. At the west…well, I can't really remember."

"Ha, ha, very funny," Leah scoffed.

"I'll get you a map of the layout when you're able to explore. Until then, your adoring fans will have to visit you in your room."

"Luckily, I don't have a lot of fans. These are the only clothes I own. I forgot to bring home my orange D.O.C. lounging suit."

"Ugh," Caleb groaned. "Our gardener's old shirts would be better."

"I'd rather wear your shirts," Leah giggled.

"Sorry honey, I've made other plans. I gave my mother a credit card and your sizes. Don't worry though, she has great taste and is a shopping monster that needs to be fed."

"You shouldn't have done that."

"Why?"

"You shouldn't spend all that money on me."

Caleb stopped her wheelchair in the hallway and knelt beside her. "You shouldn't have had to bear so much of the burden alone. I left you that night because I had a family emergency. I could have gotten your information first. I could have awoken you to say goodbye. I could have at least left you my card with a note to call me. I've kicked myself in the ass a million times."

Leah's voice dropped below a whisper. "So, all this is an apology."

"I do apologize, but that's not what this is about. This is about indulging the mother of my child and the most beautiful woman I know."

"When will she be here? Are we sharing a room?" Caleb loved her glib humor. "Your parents are going to think I'm a gold-digger."

"My parents love you. I do have to admit though, the more I picture you wearing my shirts, the more I like it."

"We'll save that for the days we do laundry."

"Laundry? I think that's on the east end, ground floor, although, I've never actually seen it." He looked down both sides of the west hall, but didn't see an open door being prepared for her. "I guess I'll take you to my suite until I find out what my mother's up to. And no more talk about wearing my shirts. I picture you looking damned sexy in them and I can't take advantage when you're blind."

"What's the matter, Cal? I could always use the brail method."

"Just stop," he groaned. "The doctor said no funny business."

"There's nothing funny about brail."

After stepping inside his door, Caleb looked back into the hallway. He wasn't sure he'd entered the right room.

"What the hell?" he exclaimed. His desk had been replaced by a crib. There was a matching white dresser where his file cabinet had been. Instead of the brown leather chair he worked in, he found an elaborate rocker with thick cushions tied on with bows. The fabrics were an underwater pattern with mermaid accents. His mother's calling card.

"In here Cal," Melly's voice called from the bedroom.

That room was almost as he'd left it, except for a smaller crib by the bed and a caddy full of diapers, blankets, and bottles of baby goop.

The door to the closet where he kept his sports equipment was open. The bats, balls, clubs, and such were gone. The thief was inside with empty shopping bags surrounding her feet. One side of the closet held all kinds of women's clothes and shoes, the other side was for the baby. How many kids was she planning to dress?

"I'm picturing my platinum card, melted into a machine at the store checkout desk."

"Oh, don't be silly," Melly chirped. "You told me Leah needed clothes and that's all I bought...on your card. Just look at all this lace and ruffles. Isn't it precious? I couldn't resist."

"Does Dad know you've lost your mind?"

"Of course, honey. He moved the furniture."

"Okay. If you've given Leah my suite, where am I supposed to sleep?"

"Well," she drew out. "You can share the suite with Leah or find another room."

"Mother!"

"I'm going to visit my granddaughter and her poor, neglected mother until you decide."

Caleb didn't have time to think about it before his father came into the room. "Cal, Ted's here with a couple of people who need to speak with you."

"Can't it wait, Dad? We just got here from the hospital and Leah hasn't had a chance to acclimate herself. She has to find out where everything is, in case no one's around to help her."

"As if any woman who comes into this house isn't going to make a run for her and that baby," Ian scoffed.

"I can help, Cal." Melly offered. "It'll give us a chance for a little girl talk."

"Ted says his news is important, son," Ian added.

"Well, I guess it's okay. Just make sure she gets straight into bed and doesn't strain herself, Mom. Don't let her pick up anything heavier than the baby."

As they walked down the hall to the game room, Caleb asked, "What's the problem?"

"Ted showed up with a detective and that young cop from the hospital. He said it would be best to talk to us together."

Caleb and his father entered the room to find three grim faces staring up at them. The guests stood while Ted introduced them. "Ian and Caleb McCrae, I believe you remember Officer Jake Scott from his time guarding Leah at the hospital."

"Actually, I never got the chance to go by there." Ian shook the young man's hand.

"This is Detective Noah LaGrange," Ted continued. "He was called to a suspicious arson last night."

"How can we help?" Caleb asked.

They all sat while Detective LaGrange referred to a pocket notebook to fill them in. "I was called to the Elite Style Beauty Spa last night at 10:20. It's an exclusive salon out by the causeway. It had been closed since seven that evening. Fire Department personnel found two bodies in the burned-out building. One was identified as Tanya Carmichael, the shop's head stylist. The other carried a wallet belonging to Horace Weinstein."

"What was he doing there after hours? Was he dating the girl?" Ian asked.

"No, Miss Carmichael was seeing a guy half his age, half his weight, and ten times as well off. He's an emergency room doctor at Saint Joe's specializing in facial surgery. He'd been tied up with a car accident while all this was happening. The reason I was called in, specifically, is because I'm looking into the Fletcher case Weinstein screwed around with."

"I appreciate that," Caleb stated impatiently, "but how does his death, suspicious or otherwise, concern us?"

"Officer Scott conducted interviews in the crowd. The alarm company had called the salon manager who told Scott that the Carmichael girl had asked permission to take an afterhour's client. The manager described the client's voice as an older Russian man who wanted a hair and beard dye. Scott thought it was too much of a coincidence that Weinstein had worked the Fletcher case, and while guarding her, he'd been told to watch out for a Russian with dark hair and beard. I have to agree."

"So Petrov was in that salon last night before it burned down with Weinstein and the girl inside," Ian said. "Maybe Weinstein had met with Petrov, and then stayed behind. It still could have been an accident."

"Did I forget to mention that both victims were tied to styling chairs by cords cut from blow driers and curling irons? They didn't have a chance of getting out alive." LaGrange clicked the end of his ballpoint pen and posed it over his notebook. "I'd like all the information you have on this Petrov character and any associates you may know of."

Caleb started with the newspaper articles about Charles Fletcher and ended with the note that Petrov had scrawled on the back of Leah's greeting card. More than an hour passed before he was able to return to his suite.

He gently shook his mother awake where she'd dozed off in the rocking chair. Wordlessly, they hugged good night.

Belle slept in her bassinette by the bed. He didn't think he'd ever seen her more content. He grinned when her lips puckered and her curled tongue poked out making sucking noises. As precious as she was, he still couldn't wrap his mind around the fact that she was his. A twinge of pain touched his heart. It seemed like a betrayal to Angel's memory.

He turned his attention to Leah, asleep with one delicate hand resting on Belle's tiny belly. She looked so soft and pale. Her skin made him think of peach rose petals. Her hair was like dark feathers. She couldn't be more different than Brenda.

Brenda had been an athletic blonde with a beach tan who loved to laugh. Leah hadn't had much in her life to laugh about since being left to care for a mother with addiction issues. Thankfully she'd been in her teens when her father died. A younger child might not have survived.

Caleb eased open the dresser drawer to find a clean T-shirt and sleep pants. He stepped into the bathroom to change and brush his teeth. With Leah's burdens still on his mind he recalled the autopsy photos of Charles Fletcher.

Charlie's death had been brutal, but it might have been a beating that had gotten out of control. It could be argued that his death hadn't been intentional, an act of passion that hadn't been premeditated. Had Petrov actually laid a hand on Leah's father? Two hired men had beaten Ted. The guard, Katya, had attacked Leah.

He probably wasn't in the building when someone had set fire to the beauty salon. However, Caleb had no doubt he'd given the order. Did he feel responsible for Weinstein's death? No. Weinstein set himself on a path of destruction a long time ago. He couldn't accept the young hairdresser's death as collateral damage. She deserved better than that. She'd simply been in the wrong place at the wrong time with a dangerous client. She'd probably heard or witnessed something she shouldn't have. That was all on Petrov and he needed to pay for it.

Chapter Fifteen

It was four in the morning when Bogdan Petrov walked into the foyer of his wife's old Victorian house. Hearing her gravelly snore he gazed up the stairs. There wasn't a trace of feminine grace left in the woman's inebriated body. His night would have been perfect if he'd found her silently laying at the bottom of the steps instead. It would be easy to arrange if he didn't need access to her property and leverage against her daughter.

Thinking about the conversation with Weinstein the night before had caused him stress throughout the day. He'd been sloppy, and drawn attention to the investigation and court case against Leah. Getting to speak with her would be much harder now that she'd been released to McCrae.

He played the salon fire over and over in his mind. He was sure no evidence had been left. No one had been in the area to witness his departure. But had the woman told anyone he'd made the appointment? What did it matter? He hadn't given his real name.

Petrov hung his suit jacket in the closet and removed his favorite smoking jacket. They were said to be passé, but he believed a true gentleman should still wear them. This one had ornate gold stitching on green velvet with a black silk lapel. He'd had it, and a few others, handmade by a tailor in Moscow.

The thought of his homeland brought Katya to mind. She'd exceeded her boundaries. Like Weinstein, she'd drawn attention to herself and compromised their mission. Another year in the private club should teach her a lesson, and then he'd think about buying her back. She would once again be his little kitten. After all, she was the only family he had left. He checked the display on his phone. She should have found a way to call by now. Perhaps she was still angry. It was certain she was busy.

Using a mirror over the entryway table Petrov examined his sideburns and the part in his hair. The salon woman had done a good job. He looked years younger than his true age.

A smile spread his lips when he thought of the last time he'd studied his reflection. He'd had a large heavy framed mirror mounted behind his desk for special occasions. Tonight had been one of those occasions.

The stress lately made him choose a dancer at the club. He needed to relieve a little pressure. He always chose dancers. They were usually desperate for quick money: drug addicts, students, struggling artists, single mothers, or wives wanting to hide an income from their husbands. Technically they weren't employees; they were contractors. They paid the club fifty dollars a night to make hundreds in untaxed cash. The arrangement earned him some liberties. If a lady didn't appreciate his attention, she could leave and another was always ready to take her place.

Tonight's small brunette dancer had giggled when he tied her hands to his desk drawer handle. She could look up and see herself laid across the polished mahogany surface. She could see his hard, bear-like body loom over her as he drove himself between her spread legs. A surprised expression appeared when he stuffed a hand towel inside her mouth. She squirmed and wiggled when he wrapped his belt around her thin, creamy neck. Her eyes bulged with panic as her face grew a deep shade of purple. She knew she might never leave that room alive. Which of their hearts had beaten faster, hers from terror, or his from ecstasy? He'd tried to make the feelings last, but he almost waited too long. That happened once when he was young. He had more self-discipline now. As soon as he released her, she grabbed her clothes and ran for the door. He deserved a brandy.

He slowed his footsteps as he approached the den. The familiar aroma of rich, sweet, smoke was growing stronger. Petrov opened the door to the tinny tinkling melody of a Viennese waltz. Beside his chair the silver powder box stood open on the table. A cigar from his personal supply burned in an ashtray.

He looked up to where his wife's bed was on the next floor. His anger only lasted until reasoning took over. She'd hated the smell of cigars. She didn't have a clue which of his music boxes was his favorite. She didn't know where the key was for the cabinet that had stored them both. No one knew but him. Who had been in the house?

****

Leah felt tiny arms and legs begin to jerk before Belle mewed out her new baby cry. It was her first morning in a real bed beside her precious daughter. No doctors, nurses, guards, or inmates could ruin this moment. It was just the two of them. The mattress bounced and a large weight landed across her legs. In the next second a sputtering sound came from the back of her hair.

"Gah! I just woke up with a mouth full of curls," Caleb grumbled. The top half of his body rose to lean against her shoulder. "What's Half-pint's problem?"

"She's hungry, I guess." Leah worked her fingers under Belle's head and bottom to lift her from the bassinet. "I wasn't expecting you. I mean, I guess it's your bed."

"I hadn't planned to sleep here. I was watching…the baby. I must have been more tired than I thought."

Leah covered her chest with a receiving blanket before unbuttoning the top of her pajamas. Belle latched on to her breast and began making loud sucking noises.

"Maybe we should have named her *Piglet*," she laughed, embarrassed that he was still leaning on her shoulder…probably watching.

"Belle suits her fine. She's louder than my alarm clock that's set to go off in thirty minutes."

"Do you like her name? Does it really suit her?"

"It does. It's a great name. It beats the hell out of Leannette. I don't mean to hurt your feelings, but who came up with that moniker?"

"It was one of my parents' crazy compromises." Explaining her parents tended to embarrass Leah. "My father wanted to name me Leanne after a character in a book he liked. My mother wanted to name me Annette for an actress she admired. It caused years of squabbling until I shortened it to Leah."

"Leah is a great name too." She was surprised when he ended the conversation with a kiss on her neck. What was that about? It seemed so intimate, like something a real partner would do. But then she felt the bed rise and heard him cross the room. A chair creaked when he sat. Was he going to watch her from there? This was all so weird.

Belle had finished feeding, burped, and began to wail.

"What did you do, pinch her?"

"No. Maybe she's wet."

Suddenly a loud, gurgling rumble came from Belle's diaper.

"Poop!" Caleb shouted. "I know poop when I hear it and there is definitely poop in that diaper." His voice was coming from across the room now.

"Well, help me change her. I can't tell if I'm getting her clean."

"No, no, no, no, no. I don't do poop. I'll call Miss Hannah."

"You are not making Miss Hannah leave her bed and come all the way up here to change a diaper when we're both perfectly capable adults. However, I currently have vision impairment. It's time to step up to the plate, slugger."

"Okay, so you change the diaper and I'll stand over here and let you know if you miss any spots. Think of me as the line coach. I really hate poop."

"We all hate poop, Cal. I bet your parents hated poop, but they got stuck with two of you at the same time. Do you think your dad stuck your mom with all the poop? I don't think he's that kind of man. Are you telling me your dad's a better man, a better dad, than you are?"

"Yes, I concede to my father. He wins. There is no

way on God's green earth I'm changing that diaper." Caleb said.

Leah heard a soft click before her vision filled with the brightest white light she'd ever seen. The intensity of the glow was equal to staring at the sun. "Ouch, ouch, ouch…" She clamped her hands over her tightly clenched eyes. It was the only way to relieve her burning retinas, but she could still see a white circle on the back of her lids.

"What happened? What's wrong?"

"The light! Shut off the light!"

As soon as the switch clicked again, a clunking noise indicated the phone was being removed from its cradle beside the bed.

"Miss Hannah, can you come to my room right away?"

By the time Miss Hannah rushed into the sitting room, Caleb had placed a warm damp cloth over Leah's eyes.

"Don't turn on the light!" they both shouted.

"What happened? Is something wrong with the baby?" Hannah grabbed a squirming, fussing Belle from Leah's lap.

"I think she may have strained her brain." Caleb's voice was thin with panic. "Leah, I mean. Belle is just poopy."

"Lord have mercy! I've got breakfast to cook, diapers to change, and this poor girl to look after. I'm about to meet myself coming. You need to wake your momma."

"I'll be all right." Leah felt as dependant as the baby Miss Hannah was diapering, the baby she should be tending. "I'm sorry to be such a bother."

"Shut your mouth, child. I'm not leaving this room until you and this baby are settled and comfy. The other folks in this house know where the coffee pot sits."

The cloth was lifted from Leah's eyes and she cautiously opened them. A square glow of soft white light showed at each side of the room. One was in the direction of the sitting room, the other toward the bathroom. Blurs of color passed in front of her.

"Cal, you're wearing a white shirt and light gray pants. Miss Hannah you have on something long and pale blue."

"You can see that! You can see colors and everything!" Caleb sounded beside himself.

"I can't see everything. It's mainly just colored blobs."

"This is great!" Caleb kissed her forehead soundly and moved away. "I have things to take care of today, but I won't be out long. Rest in bed and I'll bring you a pair of sunglasses when I get home." She heard another kiss and Miss Hannah giggle. "I'm bringing a surprise home for you too. You'll have all the help you can stand."

As his blurry image moved toward the bathroom door, Leah shouted, "Don't think this is going to get you out of poop duty."

Chapter Sixteen

Ted rolled his old Chevy to a stop across the street and half a block from the Washington's apartment building. He had two old cars he used for surveillance work and this was one of them. Caleb sat in the passenger seat, nervous as a long tailed mouse in a circle of traps.

The young people hanging out on porch steps and ragged, rusty lawn chairs weren't only mischievous teenagers. Some were in their twenties and maybe thirties. All wore the same black and white bandanas tied somewhere on their bodies to prove they belonged to the same gang.

An ancient boom-box sat in a windowsill with aluminum foil wadded at the end of its antenna. Rap music pulsed from it as loudly as a jackhammer. What made Caleb nervous were the layers of clothes many of them wore. It was close to ninety degrees and they wore hoodies, jackets, and long, loose pants, all with several large pockets. They could each be hiding a small arsenal.

Their attention was on the church donation van parked at the curb. A plump old woman wearing a shiny black wig stood at the back doors watching two large men load boxes inside.

"That's Miss Bonita," Ted said. "She's been really helpful with this operation. Maybe we can do something nice for her when it's over."

Caleb nodded.

"Seeing her makes me hungry for peanut butter cookies."

"Talk about something else," Caleb chuckled.

"Okay, let's talk about babies. We're both dads now. How are you getting along with that?"

"It's hard to describe," Caleb sighed. "She's as cute as a bug, but I just think of her as Leah's baby. Anything deeper than that brings back too many painful memories."

"Have you talked to Leah about Brenda and Angel?" Ted turned in his seat to face him.

"No." Caleb kept his attention on the apartment building. "It feels like all those old wounds have been ripped open again lately. It's not only because I have Leah and Belle living with me. Connor's new fatherhood got it started, and then my parents jumped on the *go-back-to-therapy* bandwagon."

"I find one thing curious," Ted said. "Why does it seem like you've accepted Leah so easily, when Belle makes you feel so morose?"

"My relationship with Leah is different than with Brenda. She and I met in high school, you know. We were off-again-on-again sweethearts until she got pregnant. I'm not sure we ever grew past the puppy-love stage. We wouldn't have lasted. I know that. We were only together for the baby. My feelings for Leah are more mature, deeper. I don't know how I'm going to live in my rooms once she leaves. Seeing her at the end of the day is the best part of my day." He took his eyes from the building a moment to look at Ted. "What I felt for Angel was a father-daughter bond. The kind of love that makes your heart ache. In the brief time she lived, no one else held her or gazed on her tiny face. No one else will remember her the way I will. I can't let her be replaced."

"Replaced! Are you serious?" Ted sounded angry. "Do you think I'll lose any love for JT when the new baby comes? Do you feel you only got half your parents' love because of Connor? Every time you have a child, your heart grows to accommodate the addition. It doesn't matter if you have two or twenty.

"You, my friend, are what my father would call an educated idiot. Personally, I'm thinking you're a cold hearted son-of-a-bitch. Belle deserves better."

"Hey, look." Cal jumped to a straighter position staring out his window. "It's going down."

The donation van had just pulled away when two police cars stopped at an angle in front of the building. Their flashing blue and red lights indicated they weren't there for a friendly visit. Two male officers stepped out of the first cruiser. They were closely followed by male and female partners from the second. As they ran up the front steps, they ignored the insults from the small group of thugs. A few neighbors gathered on the sidewalk. Ted rolled the car closer. No one would be interested in their presence now.

The first person through the door was Clarice Washington. She was being guided by Officer Jake Scott with her hands cuffed behind her back.

"I still don't understand what this is about," she declared. "I haven't done anything wrong."

"All I can tell you is, we have an arrest warrant for child neglect," Jake replied. "They'll explain the details when you get to the station."

"That's ridiculous," an old man hollered from the side. "Nobody takes care of their children better than Reesy."

"Throw her in jail with her daughter," one of the thugs laughed. "Those two self-righteous bitches can rot away together."

"They all three deserve to rot after what happened to Easy-T," his girlfriend added.

"I don't want to go to jail." Yvonne tried to pull away from the female officer whose arm wrapped around her shoulders.

"Yeah," agreed another young guy with a bandana head wrap. "Leave her with us. We'll take care of her."

"We know just what to do with her," his buddy laughed.

"You aren't going to jail," the female officer said. "We have a place for you to stay until this is straightened out."

"Kiss your ass goodbye, princess. They're taking you to a group home. That's the same as going to juvy. Your pretty little ass will be kicked before supper time." It was the first thug's girlfriend again.

Mrs. Washington and her granddaughter were each lowered into the back seats of separate cars.

"You might as well go on home," Jake shouted to the small crowd. "There's nothing more to see here."

"I'm calling the police chief and the mayor," the old man shot back. "This is an outrage."

Miss Bonita put her arm around him. "Come over to my place and I'll help you look up those phone numbers while we have a little tea and cookies."

Caleb raised his window and drove away before the police left and attention could turn to them.

****

Leah woke from her nap feeling disoriented. Something was off. She heard Miss Hannah in the sitting room speaking to another woman with a deeper voice, a stranger. Was the old housekeeper aware of the danger they were hiding from? She reached into the bassinette. It was empty. Who had Hannah given access to her child? When she tried to get up, something fell. It made a loud thump on the floor beside the bed—so much for stealth.

"Lord have mercy, child." A brown and blue blur hurried through the door. Thankfully, it had Miss Hannah's voice. "You shouldn't be getting out of bed by yourself. If you were to fall and hit your poor little head, Mr. Caleb would have a full-out fit."

"I want Belle."

"I'm sure she's going to want you too, very soon." Miss Hannah placed the object on the night table and then put her arm around Leah. "I figure she'll be hungry within the next half hour. But, first I want you to meet someone."

"Who's here?"

"Well, do you remember Mr. Caleb saying he'd find me some help? He did." Miss Hannah let out a hearty chuckle. "He's a man of his word if there ever was one."

Leah sat at the opposite end of the sofa from a dark skinned woman wearing green. She seemed about Miss Hannah's size, but had longer hair and smelled like cinnamon and vanilla. There was a small flash on her face when she moved, light reflecting on a pair of eyeglasses.

"Leah Fletcher," Miss Hannah announced, "I'd like

you to meet Clarice Washington. I understand you and her daughter are friends. She and her granddaughter will be staying in a room down the hall for a while. Clarice will be a second pair of hands while she's here."

Leah felt a small, warm hand cover hers.

"It's nice to meet you, Miss Fletcher. My daughter has told me so much about you."

Chapter Seventeen

"You must have heard I was looking for you." LaGrange was speaking to Jake Scott, but giving Caleb and Ted scathing looks as well. "I see you've brought your lawyer and his gumshoe sidekick."

"We were just going out for a cup of coffee," Caleb stated. The young cop had gone beyond the call of duty and he planned to stick around to support him.

"Is that what a patrol officer costs these days?" The detective snorted. "It seems like false arrests would at least earn him a donut with his coffee."

"False arrest!" Jake looked like he'd just swallowed a mouthful of chew.

"Back off, Detective," Caleb growled. "No one has been arrested."

"What if there had been trouble, but two patrol cars were too busy pulling a ruse to respond in time? We'll discuss it in my office. The sergeant hasn't heard about it yet, and I hope it stays that way." LaGrange turned to Jake again. "I think I was able to nip this in the bud before the news spread too far. You can thank me after I rake your ass over the coals." Noah LaGrange closed the door, but didn't wait to sit before he spoke again. "I know you're behind this. Officer Scott is a rookie. He heard about the psycho you and your brother took down in the glades. He sees you as some kind of avenging hero. Do you want to know how I see you? You're a vigilante, McCrae. You've studied the law and passed the bar, but you don't have faith in the system."

"Hold it right there, LaGrange. My brother and I worked hand-in-hand with law enforcement all through that ordeal. No one has more respect for the law than we do."

The detective waved away Caleb's words. "What I'd like to know is how you got three other cops to go along with this scheme."

"I don't know," Caleb shot back. "Perhaps they aren't as jaded as you yet. Maybe they still believe in the phrase, *to serve and protect*. Mrs. Washington and her granddaughter needed help leaving that neighborhood. They needed protection."

"If someone was threatening them, they should have come in and filed a report."

"They've been under watch by a local street gang since Rosie Washington was arrested. They're being intimidated and harassed because she killed the gang's leader. I intend to prove it was self-defense, but I need their help. The only way I can get to the truth is by getting them away from that area."

"So, where are they now?"

"At my parents' house."

"I'm going to look into this, McCrae. If I find out you've edged over the legal line, I'll put you in cuffs myself."

Caleb held out both wrists.

"Smartass," LaGrange groused.

"As for me," Ted said. "I resent the term gumshoe. I happen to be a highly qualified and licensed private investigator."

"Around here, that's more offensive than

gumshoe," LaGrange informed him. "However, I was going to call you guys anyway. Something has come up that may be related to the Fletcher/Petrov case."

"Have you found out more on the hair salon murders?" Caleb asked.

"Only that the medical examiner has ruled them homicides. We'd already determined that. No, this time it's a missing person case."

"Missing person? Isn't that a little outside of your wheelhouse?" Caleb inquired.

"Not when the person they're looking for is someone I'm investigating," LaGrange stated. "Roberta Zeigler came into the station today at noon to report that she hadn't seen or heard from her husband for the last week."

"Roberta Zeigler? Is that…"

"Judge Zeigler's wife," LaGrange finished for him.

"I thought they'd left the country—a retirement trip or second honeymoon or something."

"You're half right. Mrs. Zeigler says she and her husband never fly together."

"I've heard of people doing that," Ted interjected. "In case there's a disaster, only one is in danger. Usually people with small children do it to ensure one of them is always around to look after the kids."

"Yeah, that's what she said, except they have two poodles." After rolling his eyes, he continued, "Mrs. Zeigler left for Frankfort, Germany seven days ago. She has family there. The judge was supposed to meet her the next day. Their plan was to travel Europe and the U.K. by train. He probably wanted to stay on the move and visit out of the way places. But, he never showed up and never called."

"Maybe he wanted to get her in a safe place, and then take off on his own," Caleb suggested. "He could be lying on a beach in Tahiti right now."

"That was my first thought, but it's doubtful." Le Grange counted off on his fingers. "When Mrs. Zeigler arrived home this morning the front door was unlocked. Her husband's suitcases were still in the bedroom. His keys, wallet, and cell phone were on his dresser. Mrs. Zeigler had left several messages on his voice mail and the home answering machine. That's it." He shrugged and resumed counting on his fingers. "The bed hadn't been made, which Mrs. Zeigler says the judge was a stickler about. The rest of the house was just as she'd left it with only one set of clothes in the laundry hamper and dishes for one meal in the washer. The car was in the garage. That wasn't a surprise. His plan was to take a taxi to the airport and leave it at home."

"What about the dogs?" Ted asked.

"Elizabeth and Rochester…" Le Grange rolled his eyes, "the poodles, hadn't been dropped off at the doggy motel. They'd survived on a ripped open bag of dry dog food, toilet water, and a Gucci handbag. She took them to the animal hospital before coming here. The only other thing Mrs. Zeigler has reported missing is her husband's personal appointment book. I have people canvassing the neighborhood, public transportation, and places he's known to frequent."

"What can we do to help?" Caleb asked.

"I just wanted you to be aware of the status. After what happened to Weinstein, this doesn't sound good. Petrov could be cleaning house. That means he may be getting antsy. I hope the security at your house is tight."

****

"Are you sure the house is secure?" Petrov asked.

"All the windows and doors have been locked and your wife took the sedative along with her other…medication," Ivan assured him. "Carl is watching the back of the house from the girl's garage apartment. George is watching the front from his car across the street. I'm still not sure it's a good idea to go into the club alone. I should be with you."

"No. You can drop me off at the door, and then stay with the car."

Petrov had awakened that morning to find his grooming items spread out across the bathroom counter exactly the way he did it every morning. The difference this time was that he hadn't emptied the black leather bag he kept them in. Also, his bathtub was filled with warm water and the scented oil he regularly used. He'd hooked the tub's plug with a coat hanger to release the water, afraid to get his hands wet. He found new toiletries, a razor and toothbrush in the linen closet in case someone had been tampered with his things.

It had to be the same person who'd lit his cigar and set out his music box. Someone was watching him, following him. They knew his habits. They knew his sins. What if his food or liquor was poisoned? Was this person lurking in his house as he slept?

He couldn't complete his mission and move on until this intruder was found and destroyed. He would find him. He would dispose of him slowly, painfully. Until then, it was business as usual. He refused to spend his time cowering in his house like an old woman.

As he entered the club, the muscular man stationed at the entrance was slumped on a stool talking to a floor bouncer. Both wore tight jeans and black T-shirts embossed with the Blue Moon logo. The doorman jumped up, nearly turning over his seat when Petrov entered. The other man nodded and rushed back inside. Maybe he should come through the front door more often.

Under the blue strobe lights cocktail waitresses sashayed around tables with trays of glasses in one upturned hand and a perfect white smile on their faces. They wore frilly costumes meant to look like naughty little pajamas. The women on the dancing platforms were dressed in far less, usually only a G-string and stiletto heels. He didn't know any of them by name and didn't care to.

The barmaid, Dora, met him at the end of the bar. She watched over the place in his absence as an assistant manager. Anything he had to say to the employees went through her, unless they'd screwed up enough to be fired. He enjoyed doing that task himself.

"Send a bottle of scotch to my office, one from my private stock."

"Will you want company tonight?" she asked.

"No, I have too much to do."

It was close to the end of the week and the end of the month. He had to go over the schedules, payroll, supply orders, and accounts. He'd be lucky to make it home before daylight.

As he walked to his office his attention was drawn to the customers. With sweaty, flushed faces and bulging eyes they didn't notice him. They didn't care who he was. They were only concerned with the nearly naked women on stage. The chance to graze their fingers over a dancer's oiled skin justified blowing a week's pay, dollar by crumpled, dirty dollar. Now he remembered why he usually came in through the back door.

Petrov's eye was caught by the booth closest to the back, right side corner. A man sat alone facing the stage. He was wearing a baseball cap and sunglasses. A half full glass sat before him in a puddle of condensation. His mouth was gaped open, as though he were sleeping. Perhaps he was passed out, drunk, or high. Either way, he was taking up valuable real estate and not spending money. When a server walked by, Petrov caught her arm.

"How long has that man been here?"

"He came in a couple hours ago with a friend," the short blonde answered. "I don't know where the other guy went. Maybe he disappeared about an hour ago. I thought he was just going to the stage to tip the dancer. He took his drink with him."

"How many drinks has this man ordered?"

"Just the one." She shrugged. "I've been too busy to pay attention."

"You haven't offered to refresh his drink? You haven't been back to his table at all?"

"Like I said, Mr. Petrov, we've been slammed."

Petrov signaled the bouncer who'd been hanging out at the front door.

"Both of you wake him up. This is not a hotel. If he isn't spending money, throw him out."

The two walked to the booth. They seemed to be engaged in a whispered argument. Petrov didn't care. He just wanted his orders followed.

The bouncer stood at the end of the table, feet planted apart, arms folded over a massive chest. He must have won the fight to act as backup.

The dainty blonde server spoke to the stranger, getting closer every few seconds. She glanced back at Petrov with a nervous expression, but he didn't budge. Finally she reached out and shook the man's upper arm. When the stranger's head flopped forward, his glasses fell into his lap revealing lifeless, staring eyes, one blue, one white. It was The Ghost, Adrik Sokolov, the most powerful and dangerous man in L'vov Logovo.

The waitress lifted her hand to find it covered in blood. Before Petrov could reach her, to control her reaction, she let out a series of shrill screams. In seconds, the entire club was in chaos.

Chapter Eighteen

"I've got good news and bad news and good news," Caleb announced as he came through the door to the sitting room.

"Give me the good news," Leah said.

"Rosie's trial has been moved to the first of the month. She's finally getting her day in court."

"That actually sounds a little scary. What's the bad news?"

"We only have until the first of the month to put together a defense. I wish I had more experience in this field of law. I've represented people who've been accused of some pretty shady behavior, but this time a woman's life is on the line. I won't lie. I'm pretty nervous."

"Okay, now I am scared, but I have confidence in you. Did you say there was more good news?"

"Yes." Caleb smiled. "Connor has offered to come up from Mayville and help. I don't know if I'd even attempt to do this without him. Together, we tend to make things happen. There've been times in my life I tried to get through on my own. It seemed pretty bleak until he put things into perspective for me."

"What kind of things?"

"Just things." Caleb knew he should be more open with Leah, but evading certain subjects had become a habit.

"You haven't told me much about Rosie's situation. She's very secretive about the whole thing. All I know is that she killed someone. I know she's not the kind of person to do a thing like that without good reason."

"She had good reason, all right." Clarice Washington stepped through the door Caleb had left open. Miss Hannah followed. "I'm sorry to intrude, but I heard what you said from the hallway. My daughter is a good person, but she's as stubborn as the day is long. I don't care how many lawyers you put next to her, she's not going to say what happened in that alley. She'll live her life in a prison cell to protect her family. It doesn't make any sense. Yvonne needs a momma more than she needs a spotless reputation. Why won't she listen to reason?"

"If I have my way," Caleb said, "she won't have a choice."

"Dear Lord! Was Yvonne involved in this?" Leah shot to her feet, knocking into the coffee table and toppling a crystal vase. Water, flowers, and shards of glass hit her leg. Belle screeched from her crib across the room.

"Oh, my, just look at what I've caused!" Clarice and Hannah ran to Leah's aid.

"Mr. Caleb, you can quiet that baby while we clean and bandage these cuts," Miss Hannah said.

In the few minutes it took for the women to tend to Leah, Caleb tried silly noises, funny faces, peek-a-boo, and tickling. Nothing made Belle happy. He finally grabbed the top corners of the blanket under her with one hand and the bottom corners with the other. Holding her suspended in a makeshift hammock he swayed her to and fro. Still, she continued to cry.

"What in tarnation are you doing with that child?" Miss Hannah exclaimed.

"I'm trying to make her stop crying."

"Well then, pick her up and cuddle her against your shoulder. Haven't you ever snuggled with her?"

When Caleb didn't answer, the room silenced and all eyes turned to him.

"You know I can't do that." Caleb groaned.

"I should smack the duck water out of you, boy." He hadn't heard Miss Hannah make that statement in about twenty-five years. "That baby isn't Angel. She's whole and healthy. She doesn't deserve to be punished because of what happened before."

"Be quiet, Miss Hannah." A statement he'd never made.

"Who's Angel?" Leah sounded confused and frightened.

"You've never told her." Hannah took Belle and led Clarice to the door. "We'll tend to the baby in the kitchen while we make supper. You two have some talking to do."

****

Petrov sat in his study waiting for the aspirins to relieve his pounding head. He'd spent four hours talking to the police at the club. They hadn't had many witnesses to interview. Before they'd arrived, all his customers, the dancers, and a few of his staff had fled. They didn't want their spouses or significant others to see them on the news or read a quote with their name in the paper. They certainly didn't want to be called into court. Most people who walked through the doors of The Blue Moon Gentleman's Club were supposed to be elsewhere.

The interview had not gone well. He'd been annoyed they'd told him where to sit in his own club. The police had taken him to the furthest table from the crime scene and made him sit with his back to the action. He couldn't hear or see anything going on.

The detective, a middle-aged man named LaGrange, wasn't impressed either. The first thing he'd asked for were security tapes. The club had a policy of protecting the privacy of their clients. Of course they didn't have security cameras. However, Petrov wished they had tonight. No one could give a description of the man who'd come in with Sokolov. They couldn't even prove there had been another man.

The police were looking at him as their prime suspect. There was no doubt about that after a thin dagger had been found protruding from behind Sokolov's arm. It had been shoved through his armpit at an angle to pierce his heart. The dagger was engraved with the Petrov family name and crest. He told them it had been a gift from his grandfather, dating back over one hundred years. Now, it was being tossed around in an evidence bag. He insisted the weapon must have been stolen from his office desk, but the door was locked as usual. He'd been told not to leave town and advised to retain an attorney.

There were two more pressing problems on his mind. First, if Sokolov hadn't returned to Russia as planned, where was Katya? Why had The Ghost come to the club without her? Had the person who killed Sokolov taken Katya? Had he hurt her? If she'd gotten away, why hadn't she contacted him? She knew no one else in America. Had his little kitten met the same fate as The Ghost?

Also, after refusing to join them on several occasions, he was not in good favor with the other members of L'vov Logovo. What would they do when they found out their golden boy had been killed in his club? Would they think he'd been behind the murder? How soon would they come after him?

This was the fault of the Fletcher girl. If she'd only cooperated right away he'd be far from this place with his Katya by his side.

Peggy Fletcher staggered into the den. Her hair was standing on end and she was barefoot. She wore a tattered purple nightgown and robe trimmed with ostrich feathers. She smelled of gardenias and vomit. "Boggie, honey, the most terrible thing happened today."

What could be more terrible than the day he'd had? Now he was stuck in this house with this horrid woman. "What happened, my darling?"

"The liquor store says they won't make deliveries any more. They spouted some nonsense about me making the deliveryman nervous or something. You know I like to have a little nightcap before I go to bed. I haven't had my nightcap yet."

Her nightcaps started as soon as she woke in the morning and were repeated throughout the day along with pills. She was no help finding the money her husband had hidden or getting information from her daughter. She'd proven to be of no value at all.

"I'll talk to the owner of the liquor store as soon as they open tomorrow."

"But Boggie, I need my nightcap," she whined.

The woman was nothing but a disgusting

annoyance. Why did he put up with her? "Go up to bed and I'll bring you a sip of my special cognac to help you sleep."

"Is that what was in that fancy decanter on your credenza?" she asked meekly. "There was only a tiny bit left and I finished it earlier today."

The loss of a two hundred dollar bottle of cognac triggered his temper.

Chapter Nineteen

Caleb's arm came around Leah's waist; he snuggled against her back. His soft snore sent warm tingles down her neck and spine. She'd waited a couple hours before joining him in bed to make sure he'd be sleeping. She wished she could roll over and cuddle against his warm fuzzy chest, but no. Not tonight and not ever.

The story about his past had only lasted twenty minutes, but it had been the most heartbreaking revelation she'd ever known.

He'd tried to convey to her why he felt the way he did about babies in general, not just Belle. But, she couldn't tell him her own feelings. It was his time to purge what he held in his heart. She'd needed time to look inside her own. For the last two hours she'd been trying to figure out why her world seemed to be crumbling under her feet. The truth was, she'd fallen in love with Caleb McCrae, but he was in love with someone else.

She couldn't hate Brenda. The poor woman died tragically, years ago, without ever holding the child she'd carried under her heart. Leah had come close to having the same happen to her. But, God help her, she was jealous of Brenda nonetheless.

How could she hope to compete with a memory? No matter how their story may have ended, Caleb would always remember her as the woman he lost. The mother of the child he'd lost. The woman whose death for which he felt responsible. She would always come first in his mind.

She'd been naïve to think he'd fight her to keep Belle. He said from the beginning he didn't want her. His heart was too broken to hold another child. The loss of his first was too great. She understood that. She'd die if anything happened to Belle.

She and her daughter would have to live without him. How was that possible as long as they slept in the same bed? She'd have to find another place to stay, but where? Her little apartment was only yards from her drunken mother and the man who held the biggest threat to them. She'd never had time to make friends.

In all the fuss, she'd forgotten his news about Rosie's trial. His effort to free her friend was another reason to admire him. She'd forever be in his debt.

Even his brother was going out of his way for her. The whole family was being gracious only because they saw Leah and Caleb as a couple. Well, they'd have to be disappointed. All she was to Caleb was one wild night with unfortunate results.

The glowing yellow numbers on the bedside clock were blurry, but she could see well enough to tell that it was four in the morning. Her vision was clearing more and more every day. Belle would be waking in an hour for her next feeding. Maybe she should just stay up. Sleep seemed to be impossible anyway. Easing from under Caleb's arm, she found the robe he left for her on the lower bedpost.

She'd have to think about putting Belle on the bottle if she was going to return to work soon. As bad as she hated leaving Belle with anyone, she'd have to earn a living. That is, when she found a babysitter or daycare she could trust and afford. Caleb had promised child support but that only went so far.

The Blue Moon Gentleman's Club would probably take her back, but she wouldn't work for Bogdan Petrov. The man had killed her father and then succeeded in turning her entire life upside down.

That presented another problem: security. Petrov would go to any lengths to get what he wanted from her. He wouldn't bat an eye at kidnapping Belle. If she had the money he was looking for, she'd gladly give it to him. As it was, she'd have to stay with the McCraes and watch over Belle herself, which put her back to square one.

Leah looked down into the crib where her baby slept. Her vision was still fuzzy, but she could see that Belle was the most beautiful child in the world. She was a perfect blend of herself and Caleb. She'd always be grateful for his part in that. Secretly, she wished she could have a few more just like her. Wouldn't that notion put Mr. Caleb McCrae into a tailspin?

When a light tapping sounded on the door, Belle stretched her tiny body, but her eyes stayed closed. Fingering her curly hair into place, Leah hurried to see who it was. A visitor at four in the morning could only bring bad news.

"Mr. McCrae is in the parlor with a policeman," Miss Hannah whispered from the hallway. "He says you and Mr. Caleb need to join him."

"Is it necessary to wake him?" Leah asked. "I'm sure I can handle whatever it is and fill him in at a decent hour."

"Mr. McCrae said I'm to send both of you downstairs."

"Its okay, Miss Hannah," Caleb whispered from behind Leah. "I was already awake."

****

"Are you sure this is a real house?" Leah asked. "I don't see well yet, but it seems like the hallways are endless. I feel like I'm in a five star hotel."

"I was born and raised here," Caleb replied. "Miss Hannah made a diagram of the layout for Mrs. Washington and Yvonne. I'll make sure she gives you a copy."

"You must have thought you were walking into a closet, when you stayed with me that night." Leah felt herself blushing and lowered her head. It was the first time she'd mentioned that night since their first meeting in jail. Caleb hated that she was embarrassed about it. It had been a mutually satisfying evening; at least he thought so. If not, she only slept in his bed because it was the safest place to be right now. She hadn't had a choice since arriving here, blind and with a new baby to care for.

He'd tried to be considerate, but he hadn't given her much space. He awakened every morning wrapped around her like a boa constrictor—but she hadn't indicated she wanted to share a bed with him. How had he assumed she wouldn't mind?

She looked trapped. She walked beside him, not touching, no eye contact when they spoke. She may as well still be in jail.

Maybe, after hearing what he'd done, she thought he should be the one wearing an orange outfit. How could he blame her? He felt that way himself most days. Things had to change. He couldn't let Leah take the baby and leave. He cared for them both too much to allow them to walk into danger. Yes, even little Belle had wormed her way under his skin. What he could do is back off and let Leah have more say about her situation here.

"Why do you suppose the police are here at this hour?" Leah asked.

"It has to be news about Petrov. Another poor soul has probably dropped at his feet. At least we know everyone under this roof is safe. Believe me, I intend to make sure you stay that way." He had a lot of nerve asking for her trust after what he'd revealed about himself earlier, but she and Belle's security were his priority.

When the elevator opened at the ground floor he saw Det. LaGrange standing in the center of the parlor with his father. LaGrange had bloodshot eyes and his clothes were rumpled. Ian had thrown an unbuttoned dress shirt over his sleep pants and slippers. They both wore expressions of concern.

As soon as he and Leah were in reach, Ian took Leah's hand and led her to a chair. "Can I get you a cup of decaf tea or a glass of milk?"

"No, thank you," she replied. "I'd just like to know what's happened."

"There's been an accident," LaGrange said. "Your mother seems to have fallen down the staircase in her house."

"Seems to have?" Caleb asked.

"We can't prove it wasn't an accident…and she had been drinking."

"What's her condition?" Leah sat on the edge of

the seat, clenched hands between her knees.

"She was alive when she was admitted to the hospital. We suspect she has a spinal injury. All precautions were taken. That's about all I can tell you. You'll have to talk with her doctor."

"I assume her *husband* is with her," Leah remarked.

"He was briefly questioned, yes." LaGrange sat in a chair beside her. "I understand that you don't want to run into the guy, but if you'd like to see your mom, Petrov is scheduled to come to the station at nine-o'clock to give a statement. I imagine we'll be talking to him for a couple of hours. Give me the word and I can stretch it out longer."

"Something's not right here," Caleb said. "You wouldn't be called out for a household accident. Also, if he's already been questioned, there's no need for a statement."

"I'm called if Petrov farts in public." LaGrange turned to Leah. "Pardon my language. And, he's giving a statement on a separate matter."

"Something else has happened," Caleb said. "What was it?"

"I didn't want to worry Miss Fletcher any further. She's still recovering."

"Maybe he's right," Ian interjected.

"I think that should be her decision. After all, Leah is up to her eyeballs in this case." Caleb turned to Leah. "What do you think, sweetheart? Do you want to hear the rest, or would you rather get some rest before we go to the hospital?"

Leah finally looked him in the eye and paused for a moment before answering. "I want to hear what's happened."

LaGrange shrugged disapprovingly and then continued. "A man was found murdered at the Blue Moon last night. He hasn't been identified yet, but he was wearing very expensive clothes that were purchased in Russia. We believe Petrov was involved. It seems this situation is escalating. Petrov was extremely paranoid and agitated when I left him at the club. I was called in about his wife's accident because we fear she may be collateral damage."

Chapter Twenty

It had been a hellish night and the last thing Petrov wanted to see so early in the morning, was Detective Noah LaGrange. He'd agreed to meet at the station in order to get the police cars away from his club and keep them from his house. The publicity was bad enough, but the presence of law enforcement would kill business.

This visit did give an excellent opportunity to feel out LaGrange as a possible replacement for Weinstein. Getting rid of that idiot had cut off his source of information inside the station house. Now would be a good time to have that extra pair of ears.

LaGrange sat across a scarred wooden desk wearing a fresh shirt and tie, but the ink stains from long hours of work were still evident on his fingers. His dark hair had been dampened and combed back. He smelled of department store cologne, mint toothpaste, and coffee. At least he wasn't the only one not sleeping.

Petrov had been waiting for fifty-eight minutes. He thought about calling his lawyer, but didn't want to give the impression he was being evasive, or worse, guilty.

LaGrange opened the right side drawer in his desk and produced a digital recorder. He recited his name, the date, and time into the speaker before stating that he would be interviewing Bogdan Petrov in regard to the murder at The Blue Moon Gentleman's Club on the previous date.

"I thought I was here to give a statement about my wife's accident," Petrov said.

"Do you object to being interviewed about the murder?"

"No, I guess not. I have nothing to hide," Petrov said. "Please proceed. I don't have a lot of time."

"Mr. Petrov, did you know the man who was murdered in your club last night?"

"No, I'd never seen him before."

"He was wearing a suit made in Russia."

"They sell a lot of suits in Russia. I don't know everyone who buys them."

"Good point, but this suit had your business card in the pocket."

"He may have been given the card by a friend. We appreciate word-of-mouth advertising. Is there anything else you need to ask?"

"Well, sir, we got lucky last night. Even though you don't have security cameras at the Blue Moon, the convenience store across the street does. The victim and his companion came into your parking lot two hours and twelve minutes before 911 received their first call. It's too bad we couldn't get a better look at the guy with him. We'll put your waitress with a sketch artist later today to see if we can jog her memory."

"So there was another man."

"Yes, but he was only there for fifteen minutes before the camera recorded him leaving. It doesn't seem reasonable to walk into a busy club with someone, order a drink, which disappears, glass and all, and then kill the guy and walk out in fifteen minutes."

"A professional could do it in half that time,"

Petrov scoffed.

"How would you know that, Mr. Petrov?" Not a question he cared to answer.

"My employees can tell you I'd only been at the club for a few minutes before he was found."

"Yes, they all saw you come in. They say it was out of the ordinary for you. You normally come in through the back door. Why did you break your routine last night?"

"I was checking on my front door security. As a matter of fact, I was about to call a couple of people into my office because I didn't like the carelessness I saw there." Now he would be sure to single out those employees. They had no business discussing his routine with anyone.

"Don't you usually come through the back door near your office where you can avoid contact with everyone else in the club?"

"Usually."

"When was the last time you'd used that back door?"

"The day before yesterday."

"And when had you last been in your office?"

"The day before yesterday."

"Have you given anyone your security code for the locks on those doors?"

"Certainly not," Petrov blustered.

"Yet, your alarm company states that your code was used to come through those doors an hour before the club opened. We don't have a record of you leaving. The only conclusion we can come to is that you left through the front door after it had been opened. You said yourself that your front door people were being careless."

"Someone must have guessed my code. I swear I didn't come to the club early yesterday. You can check with my driver."

"Was your driver with you during that time?"

"No, I didn't call him until I was ready to leave my house."

"Then he can't really give you an alibi, can he?"

Petrov wondered if his attorney's card was in his wallet.

"Tell me about the dagger that was used as the murder weapon."

"It's a family heirloom passed down to me from my grandfather. It's one of a kind and I hope it's being taken care of."

"Where do you keep the dagger?"

"I keep it in my locked desk drawer. I never know when some drunken fool might try to rob me."

"I'd think the .22 in that drawer would be more reliable. You wouldn't have to do more than wound the intruder. You could use the handcuffs to detain him until the police arrived. I wouldn't recommend using the gag or cat-of-nine-tails though."

Petrov could hear his pulse pounding.

"We had a heck of a time getting that drawer open earlier this morning. And yes, we had a warrant." LaGrange stood to unfasten his handcuffs from the back of his belt. "By the way, I forgot to apologize for being late for our meeting."

"I want my lawyer."

"No problem, Mr. Petrov. We just want to hold you for further questioning. That is, unless we find more evidence against you."

****

Leah stood at the foot of her mother's bed taking in the large neck brace, the black eyes, and the tubes and wires leading to machines all around. She was barely recognizable. Leah wanted to pretend she was a stranger. She had to be stronger than that.

"This is my fault," she declared. "I shouldn't have left her alone with that man."

"She would never have deserted her husband. You saw the way she was about him."

"Still, she's my responsibility. I should have done something."

"There's nothing you could have done without putting yourself and Belle in danger."

A volunteer came in with a fresh pitcher of water. "Isn't it a shame?" The woman clicked her tongue and shook her head. "Elderly people have such a hard time getting around. We see accidents like this too often."

"My mother isn't elderly," Leah growled. "If you looked at her chart you'd see she's only forty-five years old."

"Oh, I am sorry. I don't have access to the charts."

"Then perhaps you should keep your comments to yourself."

"Yes ma'am." The woman rushed from the room.

"Maybe that was a tad bit harsh," Caleb remarked.

"I guess you're right, but it's become a knee-jerk reaction. I've always been in the role of protector for my mom. Just once I would have liked to play the kid."

"The last few years must have been tough."

"Ha! The last few years? I've taken care of her for as long as I can remember." Leah flopped into a chair and folded her arms. "I made up excuses for her being tipsy when I was in grade school. She drank so much on the nights Dad was gone, I'd tell my grandmother she was sick and bring dinner to her room. After Grandma died, the drinking became more regular. Dad worried, but he never said anything. He gave the excuse she was in mourning. When he died, the pills started." Leah gave a sigh that cleared her lungs. "By then I was feeding and bathing her. Do you have any idea how much I worried while I was in jail? She only tried to take care of herself when she had a man around. I guess I can be grateful to Petrov for providing that service. She thought my dad was weak, so she made it a point after he died to pick powerful assholes. They'd eventually take our money, beat her up, and leave. If I tried to defend her, I'd get beat up too."

"That's awful," Caleb muttered.

"Well, after opening up to me last night, I figured I might as well tell you my story. So, that's how I ended up working in strip clubs instead of going to college. How does that make you feel about taking me home with you?"

"I know a place where we can send your mom after she heals. They won't only dry her out, but she'll get therapy and learn how to work a real job. She'd stay there until they were sure she can be self-sufficient," Caleb said.

"A place like that costs a lot of money."

"I have money, tons of it. I want you to be able to raise our daughter without worrying about anyone else."

"That's a fairytale, Caleb. Poor girls don't fall for fairytales."

"You're not a poor girl any more." Caleb's cell

phone rang. He stepped into the hall to answer it.

He returned minutes later. "That was Detective LaGrange. He has Petrov in a holding cell for a while. He also has a warrant to search your mom's house. We're supposed to meet him there in half an hour."

Chapter Twenty-One

Caleb stared at the Fletcher house through the windshield of his car as it idled in the gravel driveway. There was no wonder now why he hadn't been able to recognize it while looking for her a few weeks ago. In the months since he'd been here it had gone from slightly shabby condition to a neighborhood eyesore.

Ted had been here, but he didn't realize the place had taken a nosedive recently. The neighbors probably hadn't said anything because they thought it had gotten out of hand while Leah hadn't been here to keep it in order. They were used to the worst behavior possible from Peggy Fletcher. This was more than a case of neglect, though.

Upholstered furniture had been thrown outside and the cushions slashed. Piles of broken panels had once been painted as wallboards. Wood flooring and furniture were stacked against the side of the garage. Like the trees and bushes, it had all been overgrown by kudzu. It appeared that the house was being taken apart one room at a time, and then eaten by its surroundings. Petrov and his lackeys had made a thorough search for the money.

Leah was in such a state of shock she allowed him to open the car door and hold her hand as they walked to the stairs of her apartment over the garage. As they climbed they saw that the backyard had been dug into craters of raw, sandy dirt. Petrov would no doubt claim they were landscaping—only if they planned to plant a forest.

The interior of the apartment had been completely gutted. Only studs separated the bedroom, closet, and bathroom from the larger living room/kitchen area. Open cardboard boxes were balanced on the exposed beams in the floor holding most of Leah's disheveled clothes, kitchen utensils, and pictures. The only items still in place were the appliances and bathroom fixtures.

At one side was a large sheet of plywood under a folding chair and TV tray. A deck of cards, a full ashtray, and a paper coffee cup indicated someone had used the spot to watch the main house from the window.

"I'll have these boxes moved to the house. You probably have a few keepsakes in some of them."

"No, don't!" Leah exclaimed. "I don't want anything Petrov and his men have touched."

"We'll put them in storage then, in case you change your mind."

Detective LaGrange was waiting at the bottom of the stairs when they came back outside. "We found a man up there when we arrived." He pointed to the apartment. "He claimed to be renting the place from the owners. We asked to see the rental agreement." LaGrange pointed to the curb across the street. "He said he had to get it from his car and left with another man who'd been parked over there. They were driving a black Buick La Sabre."

"Did you get a chance to ID them?"

"No, the first guy said his name was Carl Baker, but I doubt it. He was as Russian as Petrov. I wouldn't be surprised if the second man was too. Needless to say, we didn't get a chance to see his ID either.

"The tag on the car was obscured by mud just like before. I have a man following them, though. I'm curious to see where they go, now that Petrov is in custody."

Leah had wandered a few feet away. She grabbed a large piece of wallboard leaning against the railing and toppled it to the side.

"Be careful!" Caleb shouted.

Leah didn't seem to hear. Her shoulders drooped when she uncovered the area under the stairs. A Kawasaki motorcycle was hidden, covered with dirt and debris. It had fallen over and the tires were flat. An oily puddle stained the dirt beneath it.

"I think you should retire this old thing," Caleb said, "unless you were planning to strap a baby seat to the back."

"I guess you're right." Leah kicked more dirt into the space. "I'm almost afraid to see the inside of the main house."

"Let me give you a heads-up," LaGrange said. "The only rooms that haven't been stripped are the study, downstairs bathroom, and one bedroom on the second floor. We haven't gone into the attic yet. The door is locked."

Leah led them through a back door. The kitchen only contained a few items: a trashcan full of empty liquor bottles, two sawhorses with a board across the top which held a microwave oven, a bag of plastic forks and paper plates, and a refrigerator with a dozen frozen dinners in the freezer section.

A stairway in one corner took them to the locked

attic. A small piece of the baseboard pulled away when Leah pried it with her fingertips. A key was taped to the back.

Inside, the air was hot enough to make her skin itch. It smelled of cedar and mothballs, a bad combination. At the right were boxes and bags of Christmas ornaments and lights, an old sewing machine, and a crude wooden baby cradle. Leah ignored them and walked to two trunks on the left.

She flipped open the lid of the smaller wooden trunk to reveal a mirror in the lid. A tray of clown makeup, a colorful costume, and a pair of oversized shoes lay in the bottom. The larger wardrobe trunk was filled with clown dolls. They varied from cloth to porcelain. There was every size between six inches and four feet tall—dozens of them.

"Can I keep these?" she asked Detective LaGrange. Her pleading expression broke Caleb's heart.

"Of course," LaGrange replied. "Do you see anything missing?"

"No, nothing has been touched, thank goodness. These are all I have left of my father." Leah tucked the smallest clown in her pocket. "I'm going to take this one for Belle's crib."

"Be sure to clean that stinky thing," Caleb said. "We don't want her to run away from home before she learns to crawl."

LaGrange stayed behind to answer his cell phone while Caleb and Leah walked back outside. He joined them on the driveway several minutes later. "The desk sergeant just let me know that Petrov's lawyer arrived to have him released. You should probably leave. There's no sense riling him any more than we have.

Also, I checked with the guys who were tailing that Le Sabre. They followed it to a bar by the wharves. It's not safe for a patrol car to sit out there for long, so I called them back in. The last thing I need is my men getting shot."

"I know." Caleb had occasionally hung out at a bar there after the accident. One night, when he'd been ridiculously drunk, he was hit in the back of the head and robbed. Not only was his wallet gone but so were his shoes and belt. He'd considered himself lucky and never went back.

*****

The stupid bitch had simply broken her neck. Thankfully, her spinal cord hadn't been damaged. Being responsible for a quadriplegic was not Petrov's idea of a good time. At least they'd induced a coma to keep her from further injury when she withdrew from the alcohol and drugs. Not that her recovery mattered, but he wouldn't have to put up with her whining for a while.

It was much more important to find Katya. Had she fallen into the hands of the L'vov Logovo? Surely they knew Sokolov was coming to pick her up. Where had they taken her? Had Sokolov offended the L'vov and been killed by them? What if Katya suffered the same fate? Would they try to frame him for her murder as well?

Someone was out to destroy him. He wasn't sure what would be worse, returning to prison or losing his dear cousin. He'd only wanted her punished, and then he planned to take her back. It was their way. Katya understood that.

Perhaps they were holding her for ransom, or

maybe she'd gotten away from Sokolov's killer and was trying to make her way back. He needed to get home and find out what was going on.

"Ivan, make sure Carl and George see me as soon as we return to the house. I want them to start looking for Katya right away."

"I'm afraid that won't be easy, Mr. Petrov." Ivan glanced briefly through the rearview mirror before turning into the Fletcher driveway. "They ran when the police came to search the house. I haven't been able to find them. They aren't answering their cell phones."

"The police were in my house?" Petrov didn't wait for his driver. As soon as the car came to a stop, he threw the door open and leaped from the backseat. "They can't do that. They have to present a warrant. I wasn't home. My wife was in the hospital, unconscious."

"Well, sir, the Fletcher girl was here with her lawyer. She's also a resident at this address."

"Why didn't you do something to stop them?" Petrov's face was red with fury. "We haven't finished searching the house."

"They'd already seen Carl and George, sir. I didn't think it would be a good idea to show myself. I parked a block away and watched from an alley."

"Did Leah and the lawyer go inside? Did they remove anything from the house?"

When Ivan looked away Petrov had his answer. He slapped the man's face hard enough to cause the corner of his mouth to bleed and his cheek to swell. "Find those two idiots and bring them back here."

Petrov stormed inside and went straight to his study. His music boxes were out of order and covered in fingerprints. The papers on his desk had been rifled through. The pictures and books on the shelves were out of alignment. Cushions on the sofa where he slept overlapped one another. His sanctuary had been breached.

From there he ran to the bathroom. His shaving kit had again been emptied, but this time it was scattered haphazardly across the counter. The vanity drawers were slightly ajar. The shower curtain had been pulled aside and left hanging crookedly.

Next, he went to Peggy's bedroom. How could he tell if anything was missing? The place was always a pigsty. It reeked of whiskey and vomit. He prayed somehow she'd die before she could return.

There was only one other place he hadn't had a chance to search. He took the steps to the attic much slower then when he'd come inside. His chest felt constricted. If he were not careful, Charlie Fletcher's daughter would be the death of him.

The door was no longer locked. A musky smell met him on the landing as soon as he pushed it open. He didn't bother dirtying his hands to rummage through the Christmas boxes. He left the crib and sewing machine untouched. They were no use. A trail of lines through the dust led to the other side of the room where the floor was clean. Whatever had sat in that space had been taken. She'd known all along where to find it. The money had been stolen from him a second time—like father, like daughter. He'd make sure she suffered as much as her old man.

Chapter Twenty-Two

Leah leaned back in the rocking chair with a cool cloth over her eyes. She still had frequent headaches, but the doctors had given her a clean bill of health. They'd said she could resume normal activities. There was nothing normal left in her life.

She appreciated the McCrae's hospitality, but sooner or later she'd have to leave. Where would she go? Her family's home was barely more than a shell now. Her mother would eventually recover and need special care. Her daughter would have to have a clean, safe environment. How would she take care of them both and afford to pay the bills?

Heavy footsteps came toward her from the open door.

"Are you all right? Do you need anything?"

"I'm okay. I took some pain relievers and my head almost feels the right size. I was just trying to figure out how to straighten the mess my life has become."

"You'll take it one day at a time. Don't be too proud to ask for help when you need it. We're your family now and stand behind you in any way you need. You're just as important to all of us as Belle."

"That's sweet." Leah had never heard Caleb talk that way about Belle. He'd certainly not expressed that much commitment to her. All he'd ever offered was financial assistance. Perhaps he was finally coming around.

"The reason I came in was to ask a favor."

A favor…was that why he was being so nice? Suddenly Belle let out a wail from her crib in the bedroom. Before she could move Caleb's footsteps headed that direction. "You just rest for a bit," he insisted. "I've been waiting to get my hands on this little pixie all afternoon."

Whoa, it must be a big favor. She'd never heard Caleb use a pet name for Belle.

"My nose is telling me we need an emergency diaper change. Don't worry, I'm an expert at this."

He was volunteering for poop duty? What did he want from her, a kidney?

"Who are you and what have you done with Caleb?" she joked.

"Umm, Caleb told you I was coming, didn't he?"

Leah slowly slid the cloth from her eyes. What was going on? She knew Caleb's voice when she heard it. She'd recognized the way his walk sounded. She'd developed stronger senses while she'd been blind. If he were closer, she'd even know his unique scent.

A man stood in the bedroom doorway with Belle snuggled against his shoulder. He couldn't be Caleb, just for that reason. However, he looked identical to Caleb from the collar of his T-shirt to the tips of his boots. Even his face was mostly the same. The only differences were an incredibly long braid over his shoulder, a straw cowboy hat, and horrific scars on the left side of his face and neck. He shyly tilted his head down and looked away.

"I know I'm not the handsome heartthrob my brother is."

"It's not that," Leah stammered. "Caleb told me about your injuries. I just wasn't prepared for…are you and Caleb twins?"

"For the most part." Walking closer, he held out his hand. "I'm Connor, the most intelligent of the pair."

"I guess I owe you, after changing that diaper." Leah shook his hand. "What can I help with?"

"I've been studying the notes on Ms. Washington's case. I'd like you to be with me when I talk to her daughter. You're a woman and she knows you. We have to convince her to testify to what happened in the alley that day."

"I have to warn you, she's pretty stubborn. Rosie made her promise not to tell anyone."

"Let me warn you. I don't plan to sugarcoat her mother's possible fate if she's convicted of first degree murder."

The reality of what Rosie might be facing made Leah want to cry. She had to help the McCraes try to save her. Rosie was the only reason she'd survived being in jail. Also, Caleb and his family were working on the case as a favor to her. If it was the last thing she did she'd try to persuade Yvonne.

"Now that I've come off as a complete jerk, let me take you and Belle to meet my family."

Connor carried the baby in one arm and held Leah's hand as they walked to the adjoining wing of the third floor. The floor plan of his rooms was opposite that of Caleb's. The décor was more rugged country instead of the contemporary style Caleb preferred.

They found Jordan nursing her baby, who was just a few weeks older than Belle and twice her size. He was a sturdy blond boy like his father and uncle.

Jordan was tall with flowing red hair and porcelain skin. She laughed when Belle began to squirm and fuss.

"Connor, why don't you let us feed the babies while we get to know each other? The trip wore Lizzy out and Caleb is putting her down for a nap before supper. You should help him."

"Okay, sweetheart." Connor gave his wife and son each a kiss on the head. "I'll be back to get Leah when you're finished."

"Caleb is with your daughter?" Leah did her best not to let jealousy show in her tone or expression.

"Oh yes," Jordan replied. "The two are almost inseparable. When he visited last summer he and Connor nearly turned our backyard into a theme park. They spoil her terribly, but it's so cute. You almost forget which one is her father."

Leah looked down at her nursing baby, trying not to let the tears pooling in her eyes show. Her throat felt too raw to speak.

"You look upset. What's wrong?"

Leah shook her head. It took a moment for her throat to clear. "Just hormones, I guess."

"I understand," Jordan said. "Now tell me what's really bothering you."

"The truth is…Caleb hasn't taken to Belle the way I hoped. I guess you know about his past. He didn't plan to have another child."

Jordan put Cole in his cradle and adjusted her clothes. She reached across the space between them and stroked Belle's tiny leg. "She's a lovely little girl. One day soon she'll work her way right into his heart. He won't know what hit him."

"I hope you're right, but I'm not going to count on

it." Belle was also finished with her feeding and drifted off to sleep. Leah placed her on the end of the sofa. "I hadn't planned to force him into fatherhood. She was a surprise to me too."

The sound of a guitar came from close by and a moment later rich, deep voices singing a lullaby Leah had never heard before. "What is that music? It's beautiful."

"It's Melly's song."

"I don't understand. Do you mean Melly McCrae, Caleb's mother?"

"Yes. Peek into the room across the hall. Take a look at the real McCrae brothers."

Leah's curiosity was piqued. She rose from the sofa and tiptoed to the half open door Jordan indicated. What she saw melted her heart. A small replica of Jordan lay in a twin sized bed under a pink comforter. Connor sat on the floor by her head while Caleb sat on the foot of the bed playing an old acoustic guitar. Both men sang softly to the sleepy child. For a moment Leah imagined Belle in the bed, but that was just foolish, wishful thinking.

****

Caleb came into his brother's suite to surprise Jordan with a hug.

"Connor and Leah have gone to talk to Yvonne. We should run away together while they're not looking."

"Leah is such a lovely girl, but she seems so sad."

"She's had a rough life. She's hardly had a chance to enjoy the baby. Her mother is in the hospital, and her stepfather is a threat to all three of them. She hasn't had much to smile about."

"I guess you're right." Jordan picked a tiny blanket from the arm of the chair and folded it. "You know I was alone with Lizzy for the first four years of her life. We didn't have much, but we got by. As long as Bobby Ray was in prison we were as happy as we could be."

The sound of her ex-husband's name sent a chill up Caleb's spine. He was an evil man who'd killed several people, including two of their close friends. Six years before his killing spree, he'd attacked Connor and disfigured him for his wallet and the fun of it. Thankfully, he'd been sentenced to prison for the rest of his life.

"What's your point, Jordan?"

"I didn't grow up with a dad. I didn't know what a difference it would make to both Lizzy and me until Connor came along. I was lucky to find a good man who loves my daughter as much as I do."

"Connor is crazy about that girl," Caleb admitted.

"Well, I was just thinking, if you don't want to be a father to Belle, I hope Leah can find someone to love her and help raise her like I did."

Chapter Twenty-Three

Yvonne and Clarice Washington spotted a video camera and tripod near the sofa. They stopped at the door of the study.

"Please, come in and make yourselves comfortable," Connor said.

A man just as tall and fair as Caleb McCrae, but with waist length hair and a deep scar on the left side of his face stood watching them. Their eyes widened. Yvonne looked away and sank into her grandmother's side for protection.

Clarice stoically maintained eye contact with the stranger. "Who are you?"

"I'm the man who's going to help bring your daughter home…I hope." He smiled reassuringly, but it was his words that won Clarice over.

"I'm sorry." Leah moved past them with a tray of iced tea and cookies. "You haven't met Caleb's brother Connor yet. He's an attorney as well. He and his family came all the way from Mayville to help with Rosie's case."

"You have a family?" Yvonne asked.

"Yes." Connor laughed. "My wife, Jordan, and I have a daughter who's five. Her name is Lizzy. Our son, Cole, is just slightly older than Belle."

Yvonne's grip on her grandmother loosened. She stretched one arm to point at the camera. "What's that for? I thought we were just going to talk."

"Yvonne, we need to know what happened in the alley the day Easy-T died," Leah replied. "Your mom shouldn't have to go to prison for something she was justified in doing."

"A video may keep you from having to testify in person," Connor added.

"My mom told me not to tell a living soul what happened that day." Tears gathered in Yvonne's eyes. "She said his gang would kill us all."

"We're working on finding you a new place to live," Connor said. "You'll never have to go back there again."

"What do you think, Ms. Washington?" Leah asked Clarice.

The older woman led Yvonne to the sofa. She sat next to her and took her hand. "Baby," she cooed. "Your momma is willing to sacrifice her life to keep you safe. I'd like to have the chance to do the same for her. She may be your mother, but she's still my child."

A tear rolled down Yvonne's cheek as she looked up at Connor and Leah. She silently nodded consent.

****

The humming sound of silence was magnified in the open spaces as Petrov walked through his wife's house to his study. He'd had to straighten the room himself the night before. Dust wasn't good for the skin and this morning he'd noticed puffiness under his eyes.

Keeping up a perfect appearance was difficult when he had to buy new grooming products every time someone tampered with his shaving bag. He felt more violated by the police search than by the mysterious intruder. They reminded him of the years he spent in prison at the mercy of uniformed guards always *tossing* his belongings in search of contraband.

It would do good to redirect his thoughts with the accounting books from The Blue Moon. And, instead of playing his favorite music box, he'd choose the loudest among his collection.

When a deep bell tone rang through the house he jumped like a frightened child. Thank goodness no one was there to witness his moment of vulnerability. However, someone was at the front door, uninvited and unexpected. Americans had no sense of decorum. Before he could react the visitor pounded on the door.

"May I come in to talk with you for a few minutes?" Detective LaGrange shouted.

"I'm very busy this morning." Petrov started to close the door.

"We can talk at the station house then."

Petrov threw the door wide and continued to his study, leaving LaGrange to follow. The detective didn't wait for an invitation. He sat in a chair at the front of Petrov's desk. He pulled a cell phone from the inside pocket of his jacket, tapped a few buttons, and held up the screen to Petrov. It displayed a picture of a decaying body in a pile of leaves.

"Do you know who this man is?"

"I wouldn't have known it was a man if you hadn't told me." Petrov struggled to control the bile boiling in his stomach. "Of course I can't identify him. What is the meaning of this?"

"An anonymous caller told us where we could find him in Desoto Park. He called from a pay-as-you-go cell phone and wouldn't give his name or any further information. He said he'd be a dead man if the Russian found out he'd called."

"I'm not the only Russian living in the Tampa Bay area. I'm sure there must be hundreds of Russian tourists, as well. Why did you think of me?"

"For one thing, it won't be the first body you've been connected to this week. And then there's this…" LaGrange reached into the larger side pocket of his jacket this time and removed a sealed evidence bag. It contained a set of car keys on a simple ring with a metal tag. They were caked with dirt. "The number on this is registered to your car—the Mercedes you use every day."

Petrov's perfectly trimmed hair and beard began to itch with perspiration. He also felt dampness under his arms. He stared at LaGrange without blinking. "I'm sure you're aware I have a driver. Ivan keeps the keys to my car on him constantly. I can't say I've ever handled them."

"I'll need all the information you have about him. Do you know where I can find him now?"

"Not exactly. He took the car to be serviced and have something done with the tires, I think. I don't expect him to return for a few hours."

They walked back to the front door, but before he could open it LaGrange spoke again. "Coincidences are piling up around you, Mr. Petrov. We'll be keeping an eye on you. Don't plan any vacations anytime soon."

"Perhaps I should speak to my attorney. I may have to file charges for harassment." Petrov held his hands out and shrugged. "Even after invading my home, you haven't found a speck of evidence you can arrest me on. Yet, you won't leave me alone. I've paid for any crimes I've committed. Now, I'm just a simple business man."

He stood in the door as LaGrange returned to his car, but it wasn't the detective he watched. He recognized the old man leaning against a large SUV parked across the street. The last time he'd laid eyes on Eduard Pushkin was many years ago in Russia.

"It's been a long time, Eduard. What brings you to Florida?"

"You've become a rude American, Bogdan. Aren't you going to invite me into your home?"

Reluctantly, Petrov held the door open to the destruction inside. The top man in L'vov Logovo was used to luxury, not exposed beams and bare light bulbs. Neither man spoke as he led the way to his study where at least he could offer a glass of brandy and a comfortable chair.

"Your standards have changed since you left Russia." Eduard's lip curled in disgust.

"I'm working on a special project. I can explain…"

"I'm not interested in your living conditions." Pushkin dismissed him with a hand wave. "To answer your question, I'm here to take Adrik back to his homeland. He was an important part of our organization. He'll be greatly missed."

"I'm sure that's true." Petrov bowed his head in respect.

"I understand you were among several people who discovered his body in your business establishment. What was Adrik doing there when he was scheduled to fly home two days earlier?"

"I don't know. I'd been waiting to hear of his arrival in Moscow."

"Can you explain how he was killed with your

heirloom dagger?"

"No, Eduard." How had he found out about the weapon?

"If it was not you who killed him, you must suspect someone who'd want to make it appear that you had."

"No one, I swear. At least, not until a few moments ago."

"Tell me."

"I think one of the men close to me has betrayed me."

"I see." Pushkin took the liberty of choosing a cigar from Petrov's special stock. He rolled it under his nose before biting off the end and spitting the scrap on the floor. "You wouldn't have these problems if you had agreed to be a member of the organization. We take care of our own. We also seek vengeance for those taken from us."

Petrov's blood chilled. If Sokolov's killer wasn't found soon, he would be the target of their revenge.

"There is another matter I must speak to you about, Bogdan." Pushkin lit the cigar and let the smoke roll from his mouth. "The L'vov Logovo paid you a large amount of money for merchandise they've yet to receive. Where is the woman?"

"I-I-I don't know, Eduard. She was given to Adrik days before he was found and hasn't been heard from since. I'm afraid she's been taken prisoner or killed."

"It seems you don't know a lot of what goes on beneath your nose, Bogdan." Pushkin ground the nearly whole cigar into an ugly stub. "I'll expect you to deliver the woman to me personally within thirty days. You've heard how I can be when I'm disappointed."

Hours had passed. The room was dark, but Petrov didn't turn on a light. He was deep in thought about which of his men had betrayed him, what could have happened to Katya, and how he could keep the L'vov Logovo from blaming him for The Ghost's death.

He ignored the doorbell and the knocking. Soon a key turned in the lock.

"Are you here, Mr. Petrov? Has something happened?"

He didn't answer. After sitting in silence for so long he had to clear his throat to regain the strength in his voice.

"There you are." Ivan walked to the center of the room. "The car has been fully serviced. Would you like to go anywhere, sir?"

"I have to finish this month's bookkeeping. I think it best to stay in tonight."

"Will you want to visit your wife?"

"Is that judgment I hear in your voice, Ivan? I'll decide when to sit by her bedside. You'll just drive my car when I tell you to."

"Sorry, sir." Ivan hung his head. Was it to keep from showing embarrassment, anger, or duplicity?

"Ivan, there are two sets of keys to my car, is that right?"

"Yes, sir." Ivan pulled the ones he'd just used from his pants pocket. "These are always with me."

"And the other set?" Petrov asked.

"They're kept locked in your desk at the club, sir."

The same locked drawer where his dagger had been. Petrov remembered seeing them, now that Ivan reminded him. Chances were Sokolov's killer had removed the keys. They were providing the police with physical evidence against him.

It was time for him to disappear, to start a new life in another place. There were only two things holding him back. One: he had to find his dear cousin and avenge any harm that may have come to her. And two: he couldn't let the Fletcher girl get away with what she'd done to him. She now owed him more than the money her father had taken. She would also pay in blood.

Chapter Twenty-Four

Leah called the hospital three times throughout the day to check on her mother's condition. According to the nurses, nothing had changed. Each time she called, she spoke to a different person and it seemed as though they were reading from a script. *"Mrs. Petrov is in stable condition. She's receiving nourishment and healing as expected."*

If only Leah could speak directly to the doctor, but he was too busy to take her calls. She'd been responsible for her mother for a long time, and now she was an outsider. She couldn't sit at her mother's bedside when Bogdan Petrov was free to walk in at any moment. He was too much of a threat. It made Leah want to scream. She was sure he'd been responsible for her mother's fall, but there was no way to prove it. Her mother would eventually be awakened from the coma, but would she admit Petrov had abused her? What if she'd been too drunk to know, or too drugged to remember?

Between calls, she'd searched the internet and newspapers for job listings, apartments, and day care centers.

She'd need to do more research before trusting anyone with Belle. The McCraes were lucky to have Miss Hannah. She took care of any domestic needs they had throughout the day or night. She'd been a godsend while Leah waited for her sight to return. There'd been several times when she wished her mother could be more like Miss Hannah: nurturing, caring, and competent. However, she'd overheard Miss Hannah tell Clarice that she planned to help Connor's family for a while after they went home. It was another reason to envy Jordan and her children.

Did they realize how lucky they were to have a man like Connor to love and look after them? He was a good man, everything she wished Caleb could be. It didn't matter what tragedy he'd been through in the past, he was completely devoted to their welfare and happiness. Watching Connor with his children made Leah miss her own father all over again.

At least she'd had a father who loved her for a short time. That was more than Yvonne ever had. Some people say growing up without a male influence makes you stronger. Maybe it just makes you harder.

After hearing the girl's account of what her mother had done to protect her, Leah had a new respect for her old cellmate, Rosie. She prayed Caleb and Connor would be able to help her. They'd been working hard on her case with their father and friend, Ted.

"Ted will be picking up Miss Bonita in the morning." Caleb was saying to Connor as the two men entered the room. "I think he's hoping for cookies.

"We've put her on the witness list, but I don't want to use her unless Yvonne's testimony gets shaky."

"The jurors seem like a nice bunch of people. I just hope Rosie doesn't get defensive and scare them," Connor remarked.

"She'll feel more confident seeing a friend in the courtroom. Let's hope it softens her anger after she finds out her daughter is there," Caleb added.

"She'll have more than one friend for moral support," Leah announced. "I plan to be there, too. After all she did for me, I owe her at least that much."

"I don't think that's a good idea. Petrov is just waiting to find you out in the open."

"I can't see my mother because of him. Now you're telling me I can't go to a heavily guarded courthouse? When did you become my keeper?"

"When I got you out of jail and brought you here."

"Whoa, wait a minute, Cal," Connor interrupted. "Maybe we can arrange something."

"Don't try to change my mind, Con. We don't know where Petrov or his thugs are going to be. I don't want to put everyone at risk if he decides to go for her. My focus needs to be on Rosie tomorrow."

"If I'm such a problem, maybe I should find somewhere else to stay!" Leah shouted.

"Don't be ridiculous. If you had anywhere else to go, you'd have already left."

"Ridiculous?" Leah was white hot with fury. "I'll pack our things now. I'd rather live on a bench at the bus station than stay here another minute."

"Leah!"

"Shut up, Caleb, just shut up." Connor stepped between them. "If you let her leave with that baby, I'll hold you responsible for what happens to them."

"Why not?" Caleb scoffed. "After a single night of sex I'm completely responsible for her. She decided to have a baby, without my knowledge, and I'm responsible for her too. She gets thrown in jail, and who has to take care of that? Me, that's who. Now, I'm responsible for her cellmate. Not to mention her booze-guzzling, pill-popping mother who married the ex-con who murdered her sticky-fingered husband. Look who's sitting on top that shit pile. Me."

"Tell us how you really feel, Caleb." Leah stomped into the bedroom and slammed the door. She found a suitcase in the top of Caleb's closet and threw it on the bed. She and Belle wouldn't be a burden to him any longer. The only thing she'd had left besides Belle was her pride. That was gone now, too. How would the great Caleb McCrae feel if his high society friends found out he had a daughter in a homeless shelter?

Diapers were the only thing she grabbed before Belle began wailing.

****

"So," declared Connor. "This is what an asshole looks like. It makes me embarrassed to be your twin."

"Damn!" When the door slammed behind Connor, Caleb walked to where his desk used to be. He'd always kept a bottle of whiskey in the bottom drawer. Instead, Belle's dresser stood in front of him with a picture of her and Leah in a silver frame.

The pressure had finally built to the point where he'd spouted off everything he knew would hurt Leah. Just like Petrov, he'd made her his target.

Didn't she understand that he was trying to protect her? She was safe behind locked gates here...just like in jail.

What had he done? She hadn't been outside these walls since leaving the hospital. She hadn't even seen what the exterior of the house looked like. He'd stripped her of her freedom, taken away her choices. He'd vowed not to do that anymore.

"Caleb." He turned to see Leah standing in the

doorway with the baby in her arms. Belle was crying and Leah looked like she was close to doing the same. "Something's wrong with her. She has a rash from head to toe. I don't know what to do."

Minutes later, all the women in the house except Hannah were gathered around the bedroom bassinette. She was downstairs making tea to calm everyone. The men paced the sitting room floor. Whenever Caleb came close to Connor he avoided eye contact. Ted was still there after the meeting regarding Rosie's trial. He was the first to break the masculine silence.

"She's too young to have measles, but that's sure what it looks like. Besides that, her temperature is fine. I'm sure a fever is one of the symptoms."

"No fever, you say?" Marcus followed Hannah into the room with a black backpack over one shoulder and the tray of tea, cups, and cookies. He set the tray on the table in the center of the room. "Let me see what's going on."

Marcus patiently examined the fussy baby from top to bottom while everyone hovered around him. It wouldn't have surprised Caleb if a halo appeared over his head and wings sprouted from his back.

"What was Belle doing before her nap today?" Marcus asked Leah.

"I don't know? I took a shower, used the pump, and then went downstairs to label and refrigerate the milk. When I returned she was sleeping. I was only gone about an hour. Miss Clarice was watching all the children the whole time."

"Cole was sleeping in the crib out there." Clarice pointed to the sitting room. "Lizzy took her nap on this big bed near Belle."

"She started to wake up one time," Lizzy told him. "Miss C. was checking on Cole so I put my blanky over her and she fell right back to sleep. Do you want me to get my blanky so we can put it back on her now?"

"What blanky?" Jordan asked her little girl.

"The purple one. I got it out of my tree house before we came, just in case we needed it. I didn't know if we'd have enough for two babies."

"I thought that purple blanket belonged to Belle," Clarice groaned.

Marcus directed his next question to Connor. "What kind of tree is your tree house set in?"

"It's an elm," he replied.

"There we go." Marcus picked Belle up from her bassinette. "She's allergic to elm pollen. Change her bedding and give her a bath." He wagged a finger at Lizzy. "From now on, tree house blankies stay outside until they get washed."

Everyone had a quick cup of tea and a good laugh before returning to their own rooms.

While Leah bathed Belle, Caleb removed the diapers from his suitcase. He filled it, instead, with underwear, socks, ties and a few shirts. He took a couple of suits from his closet and carried it across the hallway to a guest room.

Chapter Twenty-Five

The tension in the courtroom felt like a pressure cooker waiting to blow. Caleb would be going head-to-head with Randall Lowry. The same man he'd had to fight for Leah's freedom. Adding to the stress, two rows of gang members sat behind the prosecutor's table to see that Easy-T was avenged. They'd been searched for weapons, but they were a threat nonetheless. It wasn't the type of situation Caleb was used to in his usual cases. It was the last thing he wanted to face after a sleepless night.

Their glares, whispered comments, and rude gestures were directed at the row behind him and Connor. He turned to see Ted and his father, Ian, sitting protectively at each end of the seats. Between them were Miss Bonita, the old man from her apartment building, Clarice, Yvonne, and Leah.

When his eyes met Leah's she lowered her gaze to her lap. She looked pale and gaunt. Had she lost weight? Was she getting the diet and exercise she needed to keep up with Belle's needs? Despite the little bit of makeup she wore she appeared to be as tired as he felt. Had the baby kept her awake all night or had she missed his warmth as much as he missed hers? How had she become such a habit in the short period of time they shared his bed? They hadn't even resumed the relationship that had first brought them together. That was a memory he didn't need to explore today…or ever again as far as she was concerned.

Caleb turned back to face the judge's bench. He had to put his head in the game. Rosie was his only priority right now. She'd already agreed to forgo a jury trial, expecting to take punishment for the charges against her as quickly and quietly as possible. If he got his way today, things would change drastically for her. He felt a deep obligation to Rosie for protecting Leah.

The door to his left opened. Rosie entered wearing an old but clean dress her mother had given him for the occasion. Her hair had been styled in a thick braid that ran from the crown of her head to just below her shoulders. Her shoes were black flats that had seen better days. She looked like an average mother rather than the tough, hard-core convict she had before.

He knew the second her eyes landed on her daughter. She scowled and tried to turn back. The two officers with her urged her ahead.

"What the hell are you doing?" she asked Caleb. "You know I didn't want her to see me like this."

"I'm not a baby," Yvonne said. "I'm not letting you do this alone."

Before the debate could go further, the courtroom was called to stand for the judge's entrance. It was Judge Banyon. Caleb couldn't suppress a satisfied smile.

After a moment of shuffling papers and whispering with his bailiff, the judge turned his attention to the attorneys. "Are both sides ready to begin?"

"No, Your Honor." Caleb stood. "I have video testimony from a witness. Once you've seen it, I think you'll agree to my motion for dismissal."

"Dismissal?" Lowry growled.

"Dismissal?" the judge inquired. "This must be good. I don't show any witnesses in my report."

"There's a reason for that, Your Honor. May I approach the bench?"

With the judge's nod, Caleb moved to the front of the bench with Randall Lowry close beside him.

"Your Honor, the defendant's daughter was an eye witness to the incident. She allowed us to film her account of what happened. I'm sure you'll see that Ms. Washington was protecting her daughter when she struck the deceased."

"Why should we believe her?" Lowry asked. "She'd probably do anything to save her mother from a life sentence."

"If needed, I have two people from their neighborhood who are willing to corroborate her story."

"The child is in the courtroom," Judge Banyon pointed out. "Why not just put her on the stand?"

"That gang of delinquents behind the prosecutor's table were the dead man's friends—"

"Hold on now," Lowry interrupted. "You can't judge those young people by the way they talk or how they're dressed."

"I can." The judge wearily looked them over.

"Your Honor, Ms. Washington's family have been virtual prisoners in their home for months because of threats from that group of *young people*. I removed them from the building a few days ago."

"I suppose they're staying at *La Casa McCrae* now?" the judge snickered. Caleb smiled and shrugged. "I'll take a recess and watch the video, but the girl has to be there to answer any questions I may have."

"I want to be there too," Lowry blurted.

"Then I'll be there too," Caleb insisted.

****

Leah and Connor left Ted and Ian in a private conference room guarding Clarice and her friends. They made their way downstairs to the cafeteria. Confidence among the group had escalated with the judge's agreement to watch the video and so had their appetites. Sandwiches and drinks were in demand. While Leah waited for the order, Connor gathered napkins and straws at another counter.

Leah felt a sense of dread when two of the gang members who'd been in the courtroom came in and recognized her. "Hey, Sugar, you lookin' for action?" the shorter of the men crooned as he groped the front of his baggy pants.

"It looks like you have a bad itch there. Maybe you should have that looked at by a doctor," she suggested.

"I'm itchin' to get in your hot little pussy is all," he replied, unfazed. "You can have a look at this monster I got."

"The bitch be helpin' Easy-T's killer," the taller man said. "I think we should both get some of that."

Leah curled her lip in disgust. This was the kind of come-on girls like Yvonne had to hear every time they walked out their door. The second man's hand clamped around her wrist. She twisted her arm to disengage it. Suddenly, Connor's scarred face appeared over her shoulder and he growled like a lion.

The two young gangsters turned to run and slammed into a pair of security guards.

"Thanks for showing up," Leah told Connor as the two men were escorted from the building. "I'm not used to having my own body guard."

"Caleb would have done the same," he replied. "He does care about you, you know."

"I think he tried to care about me when he found out we'd made a baby, but not wanting the baby has made it hard."

"He's afraid to want the baby. You too, for that matter. He sees it as a betrayal to the ones he lost. At the same time, he's afraid of losing the two of you."

"You're a romantic, Connor McCrae. Jordan and the kids are lucky to have you. I don't think it's that simple for Caleb and me."

"It's never simple, sweetheart."

"Fancy meeting the two of you here." LaGrange had given his order at the counter and walked over to shake Connor's hand. "How's Ms. Washington's case going?"

"The judge agreed to watch the video her daughter made. I'm thinking it'll be a slam-dunk."

"I hope you're right," LaGrange said. "We like to see the people we arrest get punished, but from what Caleb has told me about this one, we didn't have the full story. I hope justice is served."

"I think it will be."

Leah pushed her way between the men, hopeful. "Is there anything new on your case against Bogdan Petrov?"

"I'm afraid not." LaGrange frowned. "All we have so far is a lot of circumstantial evidence and a tiny bit of very weak physical support. Nothing the D. A. would be willing to try to prosecute.

"Unless your mom wakes up and gives us something real to work with, we're just spinning our wheels."

"You can't count on her," Leah groaned. "Even if she remembers what happened, she'll protect him. That's just the way she is. She'll do anything for her man. I think she secretly likes having something to hold over their heads. Besides that, she's not what any judge would call a reliable witness. She's been in and out of her own trouble because of drinking and drugs."

A clerk called the number Leah was holding.

"We'd better get this food to our friends before the judge is ready to resume the hearing." Between the gangsters, talking about Caleb, and knowing Petrov was still untouchable, Leah doubted she could eat anything. "Let us know if things change."

"I will," LaGrange said. "Just stay safe. I don't know what's going on with Petrov, but he seems to be coming unglued. No telling what he'll do next."

Chapter Twenty-Six

Petrov answered the door to find a deliveryman with the package he'd been expecting. Since leaving prison, he'd learned to use the computer to purchase things. It thrilled him to obtain whatever he wanted from anywhere in the world without having to leave the comfort of his home.

This music box was solid silver with a deep blue velvet lining. It was just the right size to hold a box of cigars. It played a Russian symphony that had been his father's favorite. He'd negotiated a good price for this treasure.

He signed the shipping invoice and closed the door without looking at the man who'd brought it. He felt it was stupid to tip a person for doing a job they were already being paid for. It was no wonder Americans struggled with money. The ones who visited his club were the worst.

As he walked through the foyer, he caught a glimpse of himself in the mirror. He stopped to study his face and hair. Perfect. Holding in his stomach and pushing out his chest, he turned sideways. Any man half his age would be jealous.

Today he would fill his new box with aromatic cigars and enjoy the first one with a glass of cognac while he watched the news in his study.

Before he had a chance to remove the brown paper

from the package, the doorbell rang again. It was Ivan.

"Have you found the two oafs yet?" he asked, referring to his men, George and Carl, who'd abandoned him when the police invaded his home.

"No, sir," Ivan informed him. "I've been everywhere they're known to frequent and no one has seen them. I don't believe they're still in town."

"Then why are you here? I haven't called for you to drive me anywhere."

"I was watching the house where the Fletcher woman has been staying. She and several other people, traveled together to the courthouse. I followed to see what they were up to."

"Did you learn anything?"

"They are attending a trial where her boyfriend and his brother were defending a murderer."

"What does this have to do with me? I imagine attorneys are often in court."

"My attention was drawn to an altercation between the Fletcher woman and two men in the cafeteria. The men were humiliated by her and the brother. They want vengeance for their dead friend, and his killer is a friend of Miss Fletcher. The McCrae family is defending her."

"Again, what does this have to do with me?"

"Now that Carl and George have disappeared, I thought we might use these men to help us. They live outside the law and know how to use weapons."

"Did you bring these men to my home?"

"Of course not, sir, but I can arrange a meeting with them at any time." Ivan shuffled his feet. "One thing you should know, though. They belong to a street gang and they're not used to following orders. But, with the right incentives I think they'd be willing to do anything we ask."

"I'll think about it." Petrov opened the door to indicate their talk was over. "I won't need you tonight. I won't be going anywhere."

Ivan lowered his head. Petrov knew he didn't approve of him ignoring his job and his wife but he didn't care. His decisions were completely his own.

He carried the new music box to his study and turned on the local news channel. As the opening music played to announce the hour, he poured an inch of cognac in a short crystal glass and locked the bottle in his desk drawer. He opened a lower drawer to retrieve a fresh box of his favorite cigars thankful his wife couldn't complain. Lastly, he unwrapped the brown paper from the package.

An angry heat crept up Petrov's face when he saw his new treasure. The silver was thin and tarnished. Over the latch on the front of the box was a dark smudge. Someone would pay for this. As he opened it, the expected music didn't play. Instead it was a tune he recognized as *Send in the Clowns*. Someone would pay dearly.

Inside, an object lay on a bed of cheap blue polyester. It was a freshly removed finger, long, thin and white, with a red painted acrylic nail attached.

The chiming tune sounded on the television indicating breaking news. He looked up to see the scene of several police cars behind the Blue Moon Gentleman's club. In the corner of the screen was a picture of a young woman. She was the last dancer he'd played with in his office.

"The single mother of two small children was found strangled. Sources tell us that one of her fingers

had been removed postmortem."

A roar built inside his head. The next picture they showed was of The Ghost: Adrik Sokolov.

"Just last week, this Russian tourist was killed inside the club. The investigation is ongoing. Police say the two murders haven't yet been connected."

His business was ruined. He heaved the box against the wall. The dismembered finger landed in the seat of his favorite chair. It stood straight up against the back as if it was giving him a rude gesture.

Petrov drank the cognac in one swallow, trying to calm himself. His life was spinning out of control. He had to regain his senses. He was able to take one deep breath before the next blow hit.

"To follow up on another mysterious death, the body of a man found in a remote area last week has been identified as Judge Lloyd Zeigler. He was reported missing by his wife last week. Police suspect foul play. Evidence at the scene is pointing police to an unnamed suspect."

A growl rose in Petrov's throat that turned to a scream. His missing employees had guaranteed the judge's body had been permanently disposed of. Instead it had been left in the open beside the keys to his car. When Petrov found them he would kill them.

The empty crystal glass shattered over the scar on the wall left by the cheap imitation music box.

****

"Young lady, do you realize you could have saved your mother a lot of time in jail if you'd spoken up sooner?"

Tears sprang from Yvonne's eyes. Caleb passed her his handkerchief and placed an arm around her shoulders.

"You don't know the constant threat these good people live with every day, your Honor. Even behind bars Ms. Washington was trying to protect her daughter. She made her promise to never tell anyone for fear she'd become a target for every thug on the street."

"Why weren't the police called before such extreme action was taken?" Lowry asked.

"It takes a long while for police to show up in our neighborhood," Yvonne explained. "Momma says it's 'cause we're too far from the police station.

"When Easy was pulling at my panties, she just grabbed the closest thing she could find to get him off of me. I truly don't believe she wanted to kill him."

"Do you understand what his intentions were?" the judge asked in a gentle voice.

"You don't grow up in our part of town without knowing those kinds of things, Mr. Judge. My grandma has just as much trouble as me and momma, but she is a good looking woman."

"Don't you have a father to look out for you?"

"No, sir. My daddy didn't want me and Momma, but she says that's okay, she loves me enough for two and we get by just the same."

Caleb had a sudden image of Leah with a curly haired teenager to raise on her own. He'd see to it that they had more than enough to get by, but how would she explain his absence? It shamed him to think that Belle would tell people she was unwanted. Would Leah be able to protect her from men like Easy-T? He hoped she found a good man to rely on, like Jordan suggested. Why was he having trouble swallowing?

"Mr. McCrae, are you still with us?"

"Yes, your Honor."

"What happens to this family when they leave here today?"

"Well, Ms. Washington will need a new job and a decent place to live. They can stay with us until that can be arranged."

"My momma can do anything, Mr. Judge," Yvonne bragged. "She's been taking business school on the computer and makes real good grades."

"I hope you'll follow her example, young lady," the judge replied. "You can do anything too, if you work hard."

"Does this mean you're dismissing the case, your Honor?" Lowry asked.

"I don't see that we have a case, Randall."

After the prosecutor left the room, Judge Banyon turned to Caleb. "If you tried hard enough you could clean out our jail, McCrae. Are there any other cases you're thinking of having overturned?"

"Not at this time, your Honor." Caleb smiled.

Chapter Twenty-Seven

It seemed like every time Leah had her back turned, Belle grew a little more. However, tonight she'd put her in the full size crib in the sitting room. The extra space made her look tiny again. It was time to take down the bassinet by the bed and start relying on the baby monitor to wake her up for feedings. Or, maybe she'd leave it alone until she saw how the crib worked out.

Not tending to the baby in bed would help Caleb sleep better before he left for work. But, Caleb wasn't in her bed any more. He was across the hall sleeping while she walked the floor.

Her sleeplessness didn't have anything to do with him. She simply had a lot on her mind. Last night she worried about Rosie's trial and Yvonne's testimony. Belle's allergic reaction to Lizzy's blanket had wound up her nerves.

Today had been full of activity with the trial and bringing Rosie home to her family. Another room had to be made up for her, and Leah insisted on helping.

Miss Hannah and Mrs. McCrae served a special meal of all Rosie's favorite foods. Leah had probably eaten too much.

Connor's family was preparing to leave for home in the morning and Miss Hannah was going with them for a while. Clarice had agreed to take over her responsibilities. Leah would miss Connor's unquestioning friendship and Jordan's parenting tips. Miss Hannah had been like a mother to her. Would she and Belle still be here when the old woman returned? Belle was a McCrae. She'd always be welcome in this house, but their hospitality wouldn't include her.

Where would she find a safe, affordable place to take Belle when they left? She had her mother to consider too. Surely the police would find something to arrest Petrov for, but her mother's house was beyond repair.

If only she had someone to talk to.

Leah found herself pacing the floor between Caleb's suite and the room he now slept in. Her door was open so she could hear the baby if she woke. To her surprise, Caleb's door opened too. He leaned against the frame in his low riding, blue plaid sleep pants, no shirt or shoes. "Can't sleep?"

Leah's mouth watered at the sight of his wide chest and ripped abs. She shook her head. "Sorry I woke you."

"You didn't," he said. Both hands came up to smooth his hair into place. The muscles in his arms added to the sexual tension that was quickly taking over her thoughts. "Is there anything I can do to help?"

Leah didn't know what to say. *Hell yes* seemed a little forward.

Caleb took her hand and led her back to the sitting room. He closed the door, and glanced at the crib. His expression when he turned back to her was curious.

"You're wearing my shirt," he whispered.

"Do you mind?"

"Hell no." He began unbuttoning the shirt.

"Maybe, if I lay down with you it would help you sleep."

She didn't have a chance to answer before he drew her into a long deep kiss. All she had on under the crisp white dress shirt were the red silk panties he'd bought her. He softly growled his approval as his hands covered her bottom. When he lifted her she wrapped her legs around his waist. He carried her to the bed and closed the door before he removed two condoms from the nightstand drawer.

"The first one is for me, because I'm a selfish bastard on my last ounce of control. After that, it's all about you."

Leah remembered what it was like to have his attention fully on her. He kicked away his pants and rolled on the condom before joining her on the bed. After removing her panties he placed a kiss on her belly.

"Oh God," she groaned, crossing her arms over her chest. "My breast is leaking."

He pulled her arms to her sides and grinned at her embarrassment. He licked the single trail of milk back to the tip of her nipple and then tugged it with his lips. "I can handle it."

His teeth clenched as he sank slowly inside her and paused halfway. "Are you okay?"

"I can handle it." She laughed.

****

Petrov hadn't known that all-night taco stands existed. He'd never eaten a taco and if the foul smelling atmosphere was any indication of the way they tasted, he never would. Thankfully, the seating area was outside.

The cars that drove by were brightly painted and low to the ground. Chrome wheels spun making the tires appear to always be in motion, even when standing still. His entire body pulsed with the earsplitting music that poured out of them...if you could call it music. Mostly it was a loud bass drum accompanying a monotone voice that spoke gibberish with bad language sprinkled in. The only variation was that the words were sometimes in Spanish.

Fifteen minutes had gone by and he'd already seen three fights, one between two working prostitutes vying for the same corner, and a purse-snatcher knocking an old woman to the ground. When Ivan had tried to help her up, she kicked and cursed at him. It was hard to believe he only lived a few blocks away.

Two young men flopped in seats on either side of him. Both wore hoodies and black on white bandanas. They removed greasy white paper from around rolled tortillas with black sludge oozing from the ends. The larger man grunted one word, "Yo."

Petrov glared at Ivan sitting across from him.

"These are the two gentlemen I was telling you about," Ivan admitted.

"Gentlemen," the slimmer one repeated with his mouth full. "Yeah, that's us. My name is Killa-K."

"Killa-K." Petrov tried out the ridiculous nickname. "If I were to write you a check in the name Killa-K, could you cash it?"

"We don't got no bank account," the fat man said. "We work for cash only."

"I see," Petrov snarled. "What, pray tell, is your name?"

"It ain't Pray Tell," the man answered. "I'm called

Tug."

"I told Mr. Petrov about your run-in with Ms. Fletcher and her friend at the courthouse," Ivan said.

"Yeah, well, if Ms. Fletcher hadn't been in the courthouse, she'd a been riding my dick." Killa laughed.

"Yeah, and I'd of had my gun and popped her friend right in his ugly face," said Tug.

"Mr. Petrov is considering giving the two of you some side work for extra money."

"We can always use extra money." Tug licked the excess sludge from his fingers. "Not that we don't have a lot of money already."

"I ain't gonna do no kinky shit, though," Killa added.

"It involves Ms. Fletcher, the lady you seem to be attracted to. I don't want you to approach her, I just want you to keep an eye on her, discreetly, and call Ivan with her location if she leaves her house."

"I'll keep more than an eye on her," Killa laughed.

"Not until I'm finished with her," Petrov bellowed. "I'll give you the address where she's staying. You'll have to come up with a vehicle. Do you have a cell phone?"

"I'll have one by morning, but if you expect us to blow a whole day, it'll cost you a hunnerd bucks."

"Yeah, a hunnerd bucks every day we work for you," Tug added.

Petrov nearly laughed. These two idiots had no idea how much money they'd just given up. "I guess I can manage that. Just remember, you don't touch her until I say so, otherwise, you won't get a cent."

Chapter Twenty-Eight

It seemed a little weird, feeding Leah breakfast while she sat naked with the baby at her breast, but she was happier than Caleb had ever seen her. They'd all three slept for a solid six hours. That was a lot for a new mother and baby, and considering he'd adjusted to their schedule, he felt well rested.

"What kind of omelet is this?"

"I like to call it, the Caleb McCrae Refrigerator omelet. It has anything in it I find in the refrigerator. Today we have cheese, dried tomatoes, mushrooms, and a little bit of chopped chives." He let her take a bite of his bacon, and then popped the last of the piece into his mouth. "Miss Hannah made the guava jelly with her own two hands. It's always been my favorite."

"I think everything Miss Hannah does is your favorite. Has she always spoiled you?"

"She was a hard taskmaster when we were growing up, but she was always first to kiss our boo-boos. I just hope I get out of the house before she sees the mess I left in her kitchen."

"Bad boy," Leah cooed in her sexy voice.

She put the baby in the bedside bassinet and crawled out of bed. Damn, her body looked amazing for someone who'd housed another human being inside herself for almost nine months.

"What do you plan to do with your day?"

"Not too much," Caleb said. "We have our financial meeting scheduled for nine o'clock, and then I have a luncheon at twelve with a child advocacy group. By two, I'll be at the women's shelter where I do most of my pro bono work."

"That's so nice." She smoothed her hand over his rough beard. "We should both be back by dinnertime then."

"Where are you going?" He caught her hand and pulled her against him before she could reach her robe.

"I have an appointment at the hospital to make sure my head is still screwed on right. If my mom doesn't have any other visitors, I'd like to see her while I'm there. It's the only way I can get any information on her progress." She wiggled out of his arms and slipped into her robe.

"I don't like the idea of you going out alone." Caleb pulled on his sleep pants.

"I'm not that stupid. Rosie will be with me. We're taking our daughters on a girl's day out. I haven't been outside this property, except for the courthouse and seeing my ruined house. Rosie's been locked up almost a year. The fresh air and sunshine will do us all good."

"Still, I wish you'd postpone until I can go with you."

"Stop being silly. No one will bother us as long as we're together."

Maybe he was being silly, but his skin prickled with alarm. "At least leave the baby here with Mom and Clarice. They'd enjoy playing with her."

"I can't. I'm not ready to leave her with anyone yet."

"Don't you want a break by now? The only time

she's been out of your sight was during Rosie's hearing."

"Caleb. You don't understand. The day will come when I have to turn her over to a babysitter or daycare, but right now I need her as much as she needs me. She's still too much a part of me. She's my heart. I can't function without her."

Caleb heard the panic rising in her voice. The last thing he wanted to do was upset her after they'd just made up. "Okay, but it's just one trip to the hospital and back…right?"

"Well, yeah. I'm too broke to go to lunch or have my nails done or anything. I doubt Rosie has any money either."

"There's a nice cafeteria in the hospital. You can have lunch there." He took a credit card out of his top dresser drawer and handed it to her. "I'll ask Mom to have her manicurist come over to do everyone's nails sometime this week."

"Sweet!" Leah fanned herself with the card.

"I have just one request. Text me every time you get a chance. Call if there's an emergency. Do you have my cell number?"

"Why would I have your number? I don't have a phone."

Caleb growled as he reached into the drawer again. He pulled out a black smart phone, turned it on, and checked the battery level. "I always carry a company phone. This is my personal one. My number is in the contact list. Do you know how to use it?"

"Yes. I sold these at a mall kiosk last summer. I'm not going to get any sexy texts from strange women am I?"

"Nope, only from me."

****

Leah met Rosie in the hallway outside the doctor's office. Yvonne was pushing Belle's stroller a few feet behind her. The young girl looked tired and bored. This wasn't much of an outing for her.

"I'd still like to look in on my mother, but why don't I buy you girls some lunch at the cafeteria first."

"We could get the food and have a picnic in the park across the road," Yvonne suggested. "I'd do about anything for a little fresh air."

"I promised Caleb we wouldn't leave the hospital."

"You behave," Rosie scolded her daughter. "You run around the McCrae's estate every afternoon. You spend so much time in the swimming pool it's a wonder you haven't turned into a fish. Be grateful for all they offer and follow the rules."

"Let's compromise," Leah said. "There's an outdoor patio off the cafeteria with umbrella tables. We can eat there."

Yvonne jumped up and down, giving her mother a goofy grin until Rosie nodded agreement.

They each chose what they wanted, then split up. Leah followed the line at the cash register to pay. Rosie walked across the room to collect napkins and plastic flatware. Yvonne took the stroller outside to find a table.

After a quick text to Caleb, Leah looked around. Two young men entered through the door they'd used. Both men seemed familiar, but she couldn't place them. Maybe they worked around the McCrae house. She'd hardly been anywhere else. Still, they made her uncomfortable. Perhaps it was because they wore hoods, indoors. The jackets were zipped all the way up, even though it was over eighty degrees outside. She'd never get used to the new urban fashions.

"That'll be $22.95," the cashier said.

Leah handed over Caleb's credit card and carried the tray toward the glass doors at the back. Rosie met her halfway there.

"That girl must have chosen the furthest table on the patio," she complained. "I can't even see her from here."

That's when they spotted Belle's stroller sitting empty at the far left. Both their daughters were gone.

****

Petrov was already in a bad mood after finding a calling card from Eduard Pushkin tucked in his front door. It was a reminder that he was still around waiting for the delivery of the woman they'd paid for. Now, he was driving into the worst section of town at the request of the men who were hired to follow his orders.

He and Ivan entered through the back door of an old brick building. The front was an electronics repair shop, but from the alley it was a clubhouse of sorts.

The only lighting came from a few table lamps. Ratty blankets covered the windows and graffiti decorated the walls. Cigarette and marijuana smoke hung heavy in the air. Poorly dressed people lounged in clusters on sofas that looked like rodents had eaten through the fabric. They didn't bother to look up or even move. Heavy bass music thumped a constant beat interrupted occasionally by billiard balls banging against each other.

The smaller man, Killa-K, from the night before, appeared through the haze. "Over here."

He led them into a room at the right where they found a kitchen with dirty dishes stacked in the sink. A galvanized tub containing ice and a beer keg stood where a refrigerator should have been. Newspapers, magazines, and fast food wrappers covered the floor. Petrov didn't want to know what might live inside the old metal cabinets.

Tug sat at a wooden table with four mismatched chairs, engrossed in a long sloppy sandwich dripping mayonnaise down his shirt. He might as well be eating in a sewer, as far as Petrov was concerned.

He used his handkerchief to wipe the seat of one chair then tossed the handkerchief into the corner. "You'd better have a good reason for bringing us here," he growled.

"We followed that lady to the hospital today," Killa said. "We hung back and were real stealthy, just like in the movies, even while she was in seeing the doctor. She never saw us one time. Neither did the Washington woman or her daughter that got our friend killed. It took a heap of control not to send those bitches to hell."

"The only thing I care about is results!" Petrov shouted. "Did you find out anything about the woman? You aren't supposed to call unless you have something I can use."

"We ain't done telling you what happened." Tug licked greasy drips off the back of his hand. "We covered up so none of 'em would recognize us. Then we closed in, to hear what they was talking about. But then all hell broke loose. We had to make tracks before the cops showed up asking questions."

"What are you talking about? What happened?"

"The girl, Yvonne Washington, and the white

lady's baby disappeared," Killa told them. "They had everybody running around looking for 'em, then I heard somebody say they was calling 911. I knew the hospital was about to go on lockdown, so we headed for the closest door outta there."

Petrov turned to Ivan, who'd stayed standing by the door. "We can use this if we move fast. I have to get a message to the Fletcher girl before that baby is found."

Chapter Twenty-Nine

The sedative she'd been given put Leah in a twilight sleep. Her mind was still racing a mile a minute, but her muscles didn't want to move. She couldn't find the energy to speak. How could she help her baby girl like this? Why were so many people crowded around her instead of looking for Belle? Didn't they care what was happening?

Before she'd been put to bed, Miss Hannah helped her extract milk with the breast pump she'd barely used. She wasn't able to produce much. Her mind was in turmoil wondering if her baby was being fed. Was she being changed? Was she warm? Her diaper bag had been left behind.

It didn't help that Caleb kept shouting. He was angry as he spoke to the police, his family, and her. He demanded answers they couldn't give. She wanted answers too, but she was the only one at fault. She'd been entrusted with a precious gift and she'd been careless.

Why had she taken the stupid sedative? Rosie had refused it and now she sat next to the bed crying. There was no way to help her, not even with words of comfort. Her child was missing too. Rosie had been home for one single day and the daughter she'd sacrificed her freedom for was gone.

It was all her fault. She'd selfishly put them in

harm's way.

"Don't you be blaming yourself, Tinkerbelle," Rosie sobbed. Could she read her mind? "Just get some rest and let that shot wear off. We're going to find our girls and kick some ass when we do. Whoever took them has no idea who they're messing with."

It was the only statement that made sense all afternoon.

****

Connor looked like an angry lion pacing the sitting room in long measured strides. Caleb would join him if he had one ounce of energy left. He'd been on his way to the shelter when the call came. All he could think about was getting to Leah. She and Rosie would be out of their minds with worry. When he arrived at the hospital it was worse than he expected. Leah had run from room to room, down every corridor, stopping everyone who crossed her path. Rosie ran outside looking behind every bush and inside every car in the lot. The police had finally resorted to threats of physical restraint, but that didn't stop their tears and wide-eyed panic. When Leah fainted he allowed a doctor to give her a shot. There was nothing of use the women could tell the investigators. Yvonne and Belle had simply vanished into thin air.

Now, Leah, Rosie and the rest of the family were at home waiting for news. Everyone in the house was practically holding their breath listening for the doorbell or a ringing phone. Leah was resting and everyone but Connor and Rosie had cleared the suite. The quiet was deafening. Finally his phone rang, but it was only the shelter. He tapped the ignore button. Once he explained the situation they'd forgive him for not showing up. It would have to wait until later, though. He wanted to keep the line open.

"I thought you were leaving this morning," Caleb groused. He didn't need a babysitter.

"I got as far as Port Charlotte before Dad called," Connor replied. "I turned back."

"You didn't have to do that."

"Yes, I did. My niece is missing." Caleb was offended by his tone.

"You think I don't know that? She happens to be my daughter."

"So, you finally admit it? It's too bad you couldn't have shown her a little love before something like this happened. She's just a tiny baby, you know. And, what about Leah? You've let everyone else take care of her. Can't you show her some tenderness? Belle is all she has. Think about what she's going through."

"She knows I care about her. I was there when the baby was born. I brought them here. I did the best I could to keep them safe. We're getting closer. Leah and I were together, last night and this morning."

"Oh hell, I'm not talking about sex. She could get that anywhere. I wish you'd shed your widow's weeds and show her the man I know you are."

"I'm not the same man I used to be, Con. That man was irresponsible and reckless. I can't just run around doing anything that strikes my fancy. I have to be more careful."

"Bullshit! You're not being careful. You're being cold and uncaring. You were right about one thing, brother. They do deserve better. You can be better, if you want to."

"Why are you laying this crap on me now?" Caleb

pointed at the window. "My child is out there. God only knows where."

"That's all that matters, isn't it?" Both men turned toward Rosie as she came into the room. "Nobody cares if there's a teenage black girl alone on the streets. That's what they do. Ain't that right? She'll just grow up to be a gangbanger's bitch or a streetwalker anyway. Isn't that how it goes? Her life doesn't mean all that much when you consider it probably won't last all that long."

"You know that's not how we feel, Rosie," Connor replied. "We know what a good kid Yvonne is. We don't want anything bad to happen to her. She's practically part of the family now."

"You walked into the middle of a conversation," Caleb reminded her. "You don't understand…"

"I understand just fine," Rosie declared. "People like me are disposable as far as you rich white men are concerned."

"How dare you!" Clarice flew into the room carrying a tray of lemonade and sandwiches. "If it wasn't for these rich white men, you and your friend in there would both still be sitting in a jail cell. How can you be so ungrateful?"

"What's all the shouting about in here?" Ian was next through the door. He took the tray from Clarice's shaking hands and placed it on the coffee table.

"I guess gratitude is what has you running and fetching like an old, black mammy for these people. Maybe if you work hard enough, and smile doing it, they'll buy you a red petticoat."

"I get paid to work here," Clarice said. "It's the first decent job I've had in years. They pay me more in a week then I've ever made in a month. I know you don't want to live with me forever. This is my way of gaining independence. I don't plan to ever return to the old neighborhood. If you do, you're crazy."

"What about your spinal injury? You're collecting disability from scrubbing floors at the hospital all those years. Did they fix that for you too?"

"Once Miss Hannah's visit is over with Mr. Connor's family down south, I'll figure something out." Clarice didn't sound as confident as she had a moment before.

"Is that true, Clarice? Do you have a problem with your back?" Ian asked. "We can work something out for you that wouldn't be so strenuous."

"If you really want to make a change, Miss Clarice," Connor said. "I could use someone in my office in Mayville. It would mean moving a few hours away, but you're welcome to the job as soon as Miss Hannah returns. You could stay with us until you're settled into a place of your own."

"I'd get to work in a real office?" Clarice looked at him in awe.

"Until then, you can help out with the cooking and light cleaning." Ian wrapped his arm around her shoulder. "No more floors or laundry. Melly and I aren't helpless, you know."

"Well, isn't that sweet," Rosie scoffed. "These nice white folks can do anything…except find our babies."

"I will find Belle and Yvonne," Caleb said. "You don't know me and you have no reason to trust me, but believe me when I tell you this, I'll bring those girls back or die trying."

Marcus entered the room. "What's going on in

here?"

Rosie stared into Caleb's eyes for a moment before answering. "Nothing," she said.

Once Connor was alone with Caleb again he pulled him far from the bedroom door. "Why did you make a promise like that to Rosie?" he whispered. "If Petrov took the kids he has no use for Yvonne. We've already seen what he does to people he no longer needs."

"One way or the other, I'll make sure that girl is returned to her mother. Rosie had Leah's back when no one else could. She probably saved both Leah and Belle's lives. Finding Yvonne would only be partial payment for what she's done."

Chapter Thirty

Caleb set the alarm clock beside Leah's bed. When had he started thinking of it as Leah's bed? Probably when he'd been bullheaded enough to move across the hall. He spent the previous night with her when they made love, but tonight was different. He was staying this time, to make sure she'd be all right. Waking in the wee hours to an empty crib would be hell for her.

Leah seemed to be taking a long time in the shower. Should he check on her? No. He had to give her space. She needed a break from the brave front she'd put on after the sedative wore off.

He turned on the television with the sound low. Maybe a breaking news story would come on to end their nightmare. His eyes drifted from the bright screen to gaze through the window into the darkness. Their little girl was out there somewhere. He felt just as helpless as he knew she was. Dear Lord, let her be safe and warm.

A book he'd read halfway through sat on the nightstand. He picked it up, read the front and back covers, and then set it back where he found it. The author was great, but he couldn't match the drama playing out in his life right now.

He felt wide-awake, second-guessing his idea to stay with Leah. Maybe she'd rest better without him looming over her. Restlessness made him fidgety. No position felt comfortable and he couldn't decide what to do with his hands. He picked the book up again, just to have something to hold.

The bathroom door opened a full minute before Leah finally appeared. She looked too small in her yellow, knee length nightshirt, too young with red-rimmed eyes and puffy lips, too fragile as she gazed at the bassinette that had been moved to the corner of the room. What could he say that wouldn't trigger another series of tears?

She approached his side of the bed. Should he move over to let her under the covers? Was she only coming to tell him something? He didn't move, paralyzed by curiosity.

She raised her nightshirt to the top of her thighs, placed one knee beside his hip on the mattress and swung the other across his lap, straddling him. The book fell to the floor. The fabric of his sleep pants was thin. The heat and contour of her body let him know she was naked under the gown. His erection seemed obscene, considering the circumstances. "What are you doing, Leah?"

"I was hoping it would be obvious." She framed his face with her hands and kissed him, sliding her tongue against his, and then pulling on his bottom lip with her lips. She leaned back and pulled off her gown. His hands covered her full breasts without his conscience's consent.

"You don't know what you're doing."

"I know exactly what I'm doing. I'm making love to you." She removed his shirt next and ran her hands from his chest to the band of his pants where his traitorous cock ached to break free. When she lowered the elastic to release it, Caleb grabbed both her hands.

"No! I can't be part of something you'll regret in the morning. You'll feel guilty and blame me for allowing it."

"Don't you want me?" Her voice was barely above a whisper.

"I think it's pretty obvious that I do." Caleb nodded his head toward his lap. "But, I'm not an animal. I do have some self-control. You're hurting and I don't want to add to that."

"I need you, don't you understand? I need you."

"No, I don't understand. Tell me why you're doing this. Why now?" He let her hands go and pulled her against his chest. "Why do you need me?"

"I'm cold, Caleb." She snuggled her head against his neck. "I'm cold in my heart. I need warmth. I need physical contact. I need you to hold me and fill some of the emptiness inside me…please."

That was good enough for him. Without another word he kissed her long and deep. They held each other close. There was no more preamble, no foreplay, just the rhythm of her body stroking his, slowly, steadily. Her breaths became desperate gasps, her fingernails dug into his back. When she was too weak to hold him any longer he allowed his own release, but still kept her tightly in his arms until she fell asleep.

As he laid her beside him and tucked the covers around her he knew he'd changed. He hadn't just claimed her for the night. He'd given her his heart for a lifetime.

****

Under Caleb's strict supervision, Leah had a piece of toast and some orange juice. He'd been attentive and watchful until she couldn't stand it any longer and had run him out of the suite.

He joined Ian and Connor in the downstairs study. The men had set up desks to work from while they waited for news. Calls from their offices were being forwarded, and a lady named Ruth Ann had brought an armload of files. She fussed over the three men with the skill of a maestro conducting a symphony.

Two police officers manned telephone recording devices in the dining room, and watched computer screens that showed the exterior of the property. Security guards had been hired to patrol the grounds.

Melly and Clarice were in the courtyard entertaining Connor's children. Jordan, Miss Hannah, and Rosie were busy cleaning the house and cooking. Leah could have joined either group, but their sympathetic gazes only reminded her that something horrible was happening. She didn't need anything but her aching breasts and empty arms to know that.

It seemed everyone had something to do except her. She needed a way to occupy her mind. One thing she hadn't done for the last couple of days was check on her mother. It would be an exercise in futility, she knew, but she had to try.

All the lines for the house phone were in use, but she still had Caleb's personal cell phone. She checked the battery. It still had half its charge.

"This is Leah Fletcher. I'm Margaret Petrov's daughter and I'm calling to inquire about her condition." To Leah's surprise, she received a much different response than usual.

"We've been waiting for your call, Miss Fletcher. Can you please hold for the head administrator of the hospital?"

"Of course." Please don't let it be more bad news. If something happened to her mother, it would be the last straw to break her.

"Miss Fletcher," the man said a minute later, "my name is Isaac Hall. Have you heard from your stepfather in the last 24 hours?"

"No, I haven't. We don't usually communicate. What does he have to do with my mother's condition?" Leah asked, although she did suspect Petrov was the cause of Peggy's so-called accident.

"He has nothing to do with her condition, ma'am, but he did have a lot to do with her care."

"Please, Mr. Hall, just tell me what's going on."

"Well, ma'am, Mr. Petrov came by yesterday evening. He said he can no longer be financially responsible for your mother. He informed me that either you would have to take over her care or we could look to the county to cover her expenses. He has plans to leave the country and said he won't be returning for a very long time. I didn't have a phone number on file for you so I've ordered her course of treatment to be terminated and I'm having her transferred to a county run nursing home this afternoon."

"What do you mean, you've ended her treatment? She has a broken neck!"

"Yes, ma'am, but her injuries are healing well, so far. That won't be compromised. However, I don't see any need to keep her in an induced coma. Restraints will keep her from harming herself during her withdrawal from her drug and alcohol addiction. The nursing home will make sure she's as comfortable as possible."

"You can't do this! I'll take responsibility. Please, don't stop her treatment."

"Do you have medical insurance or a source of income to take care of her bills?"

Leah didn't have either of those things. She didn't have a job or any prospects. All she had was Caleb. She hated to ask him for help, but what other choice did she have? Worst of all, she'd have to lie.

"My fiancé can cover her expenses. You may know him…Caleb McCrae."

"Ian McCrae is on our board of trustees. I suppose we can count on Caleb, if he's willing to come in and sign a few papers. We'd need to take care of it immediately, though, if we're going to continue her current course of treatment."

"I'll make sure he's available. We'll be there right away."

Why had Petrov suddenly loosened his hold on her mother? What was he up to? Did it have anything to do with Belle and Yvonne's disappearance? If he left the country would she and Rosie ever see their daughters again?

Instinct told her she needed to get to the hospital. She needed to see her mother. She prayed Caleb would agree to her promise to Mr. Hall. The only option was to swallow her pride and ask.

Chapter Thirty-One

It was almost time to leave Tampa. Petrov wouldn't miss it. He'd always hated the area. Traffic was chaotic and there were sweaty tourists everywhere you looked. The only reason he'd returned was to claim the money Fletcher had stolen, and that mission had turned into a colossal failure. If his next plan didn't work he'd make Leah pay the way her father had.

"Would you like me to take more of your wife's belongings to the hospital, sir?" Ivan followed Petrov through the front door. "That little bag we took yesterday couldn't have held much."

"Why are you so concerned about my wife, Ivan? She's a drunken whore. This may be the first time she's been clean and quiet since she was a child, and I have my doubts about that. You surely don't have feelings for the old bat, do you? Perhaps she reminds you of your mother. One thing I don't need is my driver moonlighting as my conscience. I've given her more than she deserves already." Petrov stopped to hang his coat in the entryway closet and slip on a smoking jacket. Something seemed to be off, but he couldn't put his finger on it. "She's never worked for anything in her life, let alone done anything for me. She's a bloodsucking leech, plain and simple. If you don't like the way I run my personal life, you could find another job." He took a moment to admire himself in the mirror.

"See how far you'd get if the authorities discovered you're an escaped convict from California. You won't have to worry about a job if you return to serve out a complete thirty-year sentence. How many years do you suppose they'd add for a prison break resulting in the death of a corrections officer? Things like that have a way of being found out, you know."

"I have no interest in your wife or your private life, sir." Ivan clenched his teeth until it looked like his jaw would break. He opened the door to the study and waited for Petrov to lead the way inside. "I was only trying to be helpful."

"You can be helpful by minding your business and doing your job." Petrov swung his chair around to face forward. What he saw took a moment to register in his mind. When it did, he screamed in outrage.

The obese gangbanger, Tug, was sitting in his seat wearing one of Petrov's hand-stitched smoking jackets. Some of the seams had ripped to accommodate his size. A cigar from Petrov's private supply poked out from between his plump lips. Cold ashes dropped to his blood-drenched chest. His throat had been slashed.

Petrov unlocked the side drawer to his desk with shaking hands. The gun he drew out wobbled in his grasp. "It has to be you," he accused Ivan. "You're the only one left. It was you who introduced me to these thugs. You knew where to find them."

"Be reasonable, sir." Ivan's brow became damp with perspiration. "I've been at your side all morning. What reason would I have to kill one of the only two people we have to help us?"

"That's true." Petrov slid the gun into his pocket and crossed to the sofa. "Get rid of it."

"I can't move him by myself, sir. He must weigh three-hundred pounds."

"Roll him out in the chair, you idiot. I don't plan to use it after this."

Ivan's cell phone rang. The display showed the name Killa-K. He held it up for Petrov to see. "What do I do?"

"Let it go to voice mail."

A moment later, Ivan retrieved the message. He put his phone on speaker to let Petrov hear it as well. *"Hey, man, where you guys at? I was getting my groove on at my girl's house when you came looking for us. Now, Tug ain't answering his cell either. I figure he's with you 'cause my homies say he took off with two white guys who talked funny. If you got him on a job, you better remind him that we agreed to split everything fifty-fifty. Catcha later, bitches."*

****

Some of the apparatus had been removed from around Peggy's bed and Leah was glad to see her color had improved. Instead of an induced coma, she was heavily sedated. As she watched her mother sleep she wondered what their relationship would be if Peggy succeeded in kicking the drugs and alcohol. Was it possible to completely turn away from such long-term addictions? If the outcome depended on strength, Leah had doubts. Peggy's main weaknesses had always been self-confidence and willpower.

She ran her fingers over Peggy's upturned palm. It was as soft and delicate as a dove's wing. She'd never cooked a meal, swept a floor, or planted a flower. She hadn't had to work around the house or at an outside job. Her parents had overindulged her; her husband had made excuses as he'd covered for her; and then she, herself, had taken his place at the age of fifteen. Nothing had ever been expected of Peggy Fletcher. She had no skills to live a normal life. They hadn't done her any favors by spoiling her so badly. Leah was resolved to the fact that she'd spend the rest of her life paying for it, but she wouldn't make the same mistake with Belle.

Caleb placed a hand on her shoulder and she jumped. "Pack your mother's things while I check on her transportation."

"Okay."

He'd exceeded her expectations when he decided to have Peggy transferred to a private convalescent home. She didn't know how she'd repay him. The facility had tight security for celebrity *guests*.

Leah found a canvas bag in the room's tiny closet. She folded the robe hanging above it and grabbed a pair of slippers off the floor. Her hands scooped up the few toiletries in the bathroom. Belle was on her mind, as usual.

The police had entertained the idea that Yvonne had run away, taking the baby with her. Rosie reminded them her daughter had just testified to have her released from jail, even though she'd been threatened. She wouldn't have left her the day after they'd been reunited.

Their next thought was that she'd been taken by the gang in her old neighborhood. That didn't pan out either. The most active hoodlums had attended a funeral during the time of the girls' disappearance. The mother of one of their members had died from a drug overdose.

Petrov's alibi had held up, but he could have hired someone to do his bidding. He had no problem arranging a corrections officer to make trouble inside the jail. Two of his other employees had beaten Ted Newsome. He had a judge and at least one police detective on his payroll who were now both dead. There could be others.

The only items in the small dresser were two old nightgowns and a few tattered pair of panties. When Leah shook out the second gown to refold it, an envelope fell to the floor. Her name was printed across the front with the word *private* underlined twice. Her hands trembled as she tore open the sealed flap. She didn't recognize the handwriting on the two pages of cream-colored stationery.

My Dear Miss Fletcher,

As you have learned, I have no further use for your mother. I am returning her to your excellent care. I'm sorry for her poor condition. She can be quite clumsy, but I'm sure you already know that.

I now hold something much more valuable to you, which is only fair. You have something of mine. I suggest we arrange a trade as quickly and quietly as possible.

Keep in mind that I have eyes everywhere. If you speak to anyone regarding our exchange, a certain young lady could be sent away to begin a new life in the adult entertainment industry. A girl such as her would be rare and very popular in my country.

Another thing my country has are facilities that adopt babies to people all over the world. It's impossible to keep track of these children once they've been taken. They are given new birth certificates and their appearance changes so quickly. The youngest are always the first to be chosen.

Leah could barely see through her tears as she moved the second page to the top. He was describing a scenario for each girl that was worse than she'd imagined. Belle and Yvonne were in the hands of a monster.

I'm sure you understand the importance of discretion.

Today is Friday. You should come alone by public transportation to the place where your father took you on Friday afternoons. I'll expect you to arrive at the same time the two of you always did years ago. An associate of mine will transport you to where I will be waiting. Bring what you owe me or be prepared to exchange yourself for their release.

Sincerely,

B.P.

Was it possible to live a nightmare so heinous and survive? It didn't matter. Belle and Yvonne's safety were her only concern. Once she traded herself for her daughter, the McCraes would take care of her.

She looked at her mother's sleeping form with little emotion. If Peggy had been more aware, more responsible…she couldn't allow those thoughts. Her mom was exactly what everyone had allowed her to be her entire life.

The large round clock on the wall showed that she only had one hour to get across town. She rummaged through her mother's purse for bus fare. Could she be any more pathetic?

Chapter Thirty-Two

Caleb walked into Peggy's room. Her bag was half filled and sat next to two wadded nightgowns on the end of the bed. The door to her private rest room stood open. Leah was nowhere in sight. She must have gone to the nurse's station. But, he hadn't passed her on his way in. Perhaps she'd gone to the cafeteria or vending machines for something to drink.

When his phone rang he thought it might be her, but it came from an unknown number. He declined the call in order to phone Leah. Maybe she'd gone for a walk. She didn't answer.

Now that they'd straightened out her mother's situation, she probably wasn't in such a panic. He was glad she had something besides Belle to concentrate on for a while. And, thank goodness Peggy was unconscious. Leah didn't need more drama on top of what they were going through.

His life had definitely been more hectic since he received her letter from jail. Everything that had happened after finding her seemed surreal. Even the way they'd eased into an intimate relationship. Nothing that good had happened to him in a long, long time. She meant more to him than he'd expected. He'd gladly move heaven and earth to find their baby, not only because he wanted to make Leah happy but he actually missed the little pixie. She was a carbon copy of her mother. Thinking about Belle made his stomach ache, and a lump form in his throat.

He slumped into a chair against the wall and stared at the paper under the end of the bed. No, it was an envelope. The housekeeping staff should have been more thorough. Perhaps Leah dropped it. He wished she'd hurry and get back. An ambulance was coming to transport her mother at anytime.

The longer he sat, the more edgy he felt. Caleb was tired of staring at the stupid envelope. He left the chair to squat by the bed and pick it up. Half of the back was ripped away. Someone must have been in a hurry to see what was inside. When he threw it in the trash basket it flipped to land face-up on the end of an empty tissue box. Leah's name was printed across the front, and the word *private*, underlined twice. He retrieved it from the basket, looked it over more thoroughly, and then sniffed it. It smelled of cigar smoke…like the study in her mother's house. He'd lay bets it came from Petrov's desk.

The envelope was still in his hand when he raced to the nurse's station at the end of the corridor. "I came in with Ms. Fletcher. She was supposed to be preparing her mother for transfer," he panted. "Do you know where she went?"

"She ran by here about fifteen minutes ago." The nurse frowned and checked her watch. "She looked pale and upset. I called to her, but she didn't seem to hear me. I was afraid something had happened to Mrs. Petrov, so I checked on her."

"She went down the stairs." Another nurse pointed toward a windowed door. "She pressed the button for the elevator, but didn't wait for it to arrive."

Caleb ran down three flights and to a desk near the front entrance of the lobby. He spoke to an elderly woman wearing a pink volunteer smock.

"I came in with a small woman, curly dark hair, very pretty. She was wearing denim shorts, a white blouse, and brown sandals. Did you see anyone like that leave in a hurry, maybe fifteen minutes ago?"

"I sure did," the woman answered. "She was nearly hit by a car right outside. I guess she was afraid she'd miss her bus."

"Her bus?"

"Yes, she got on the cross-town bus at the glass shelter. She dropped some papers when she was stepping on, but a man walking by was nice enough to pick them up and put them in the trash. People can be so careless." The woman was still talking about the evils of littering when Caleb ran out the door and to the wire bin by the bus shelter.

Petrov's letter was a crumpled mess, but he recognized the handwriting from the envelope. As he read it, the pressure in his head increased to the point of near explosion. He read it again. The only person who might be able to tell him where Leah and her father went on Friday afternoons was under heavy sedation.

Caleb reacted to his first instinct. He opened the cell phone and called his twin brother. "I need help. Petrov took Leah. Get Ted and meet me on the hospital's third floor, room 315."

****

Leah transferred buses before arriving at the Hillsborough College campus in Ybor City. It was just a short walk down Chelsea to the newly renovated, historical section of town. Crowds of tourists came there to shop in stylish boutiques during the day and party in trendy bars at night. Most of them never knew that just a few blocks past the railroad tracks was an old, forgotten neighborhood where the Tampa suburb was actually started by Cuban immigrants. They'd come in droves to make hand rolled cigars. When the factories closed, the workers moved away, and the area died. No one cared about sprucing up a place so close to noisy trains and dangerous cargo ships. Still, it had been a special part of her childhood.

She stopped in front of a small storefront with a busted window. The only thing left inside was a long, Formica topped bar along the right wall and broken display cases across the back. The soda fountain and spindly tables and chairs were gone. A few faded, curling posters of sweet treats remained on the walls. A wooden sign was bolted into the brick next to the door, *Alexander's Ice Cream and Candy Shoppe*. Her watch showed the time as 3:40; she had five minutes to spare. She closed her eyes and tried to recall the scent of hot fudge and her father's cologne. Shuffling footsteps on the crumbling sidewalk broke her concentration.

"Hey, lady, you got some spare change, maybe a cigarette?" The man was what the locals referred to as a wharf rat. He hung around the port waiting to be offered paid work, but hoping for handouts. By the way his breath smelled, he must have gotten enough money for whiskey.

"I'm sorry, I spent what I had on the bus, and I don't smoke."

"Figures…" The man gave a disgusted snort before moving closer. "You're not like the girls who work down this way. I bet you dab perfume on that soft, pretty skin. How 'bout letting me have a sniff."

"I-I'm n-not working," Leah stammered. "I'm m-meeting someone."

"Sure you are. This is a real popular gathering place." He moved even closer, now smiling to show badly neglected teeth. "I bet you were looking for a Starbucks."

"Leave her alone." A tall man with blond hair and a Russian accent stepped out from the side of the building. He was wearing a dark suit and billed cap. He pointed a small, silver handgun toward the first man.

"I'm just making friendly conversation, mister." The bum held up both hands. "Don't suppose you have any spare change?"

The Russian raised his gun and pulled the trigger. A bullet imbedded itself into the brick wall beside the other man's head, sending him running in the opposite direction.

"Was that necessary?" Leah rubbed her ringing ears.

"Did you want me to invite him along on our trip?"

"What trip? I'm not going anywhere with you. I don't know who you are."

"I'm the driver you came to meet." The man slipped the gun back into his coat pocket. "Mr. Petrov told me to bring you, but I don't intend to force you. If you won't go, I guess our business is done."

Leah remembered Petrov's threats against the children. This man was her only hope of finding them. When he sauntered back toward the side street, she rushed to catch up. She slid into the back seat of the black Mercedes Benz sedan before he had a chance to turn the ignition.

A sour odor assaulted her nose. "What is that horrible smell?"

"Sorry." He smiled into the rearview mirror. "Garbage was left in the trunk. I plan to clean it out as soon as we're finished."

Chapter Thirty-Three

Caleb stood in the hospital corridor watching Peggy rolled away by an ambulance attendant. She was finally on the way to her new facility. He wondered how aware she'd been of the condition of her home. She probably didn't realize that she'd never be able to return to it. She, Leah, and Belle were his responsibility now. His life had taken some wicked turns of late, but if that was the price he had to pay to keep Leah in his life, so be it. His only concern now was getting Leah and Belle back safely.

Just as the gurney was about to turn out of sight he saw Connor skitter around it and jog toward him. Ted and Noah LaGrange were close behind. It was a relief to know he could finally voice the turmoil going on in his head.

"Where is she going?" Detective LaGrange pointed over his shoulder at the gurney. "Does Petrov know she's being moved?"

Caleb led them into the now empty hospital room before answering. "As far as she's concerned she's going to a safe place and Petrov is out of the picture. However," Caleb removed the letter from his front pants pocket and handed it to the detective. "He left this behind and now Leah has disappeared."

The three men huddled close to read the letter while Caleb anxiously waited for their reactions.

"Did anyone see Leah leave?" Connor asked.

"Do you have any idea where this meeting place is?" Ted asked.

"Was there anything else in the envelope?" LaGrange asked.

The questions hit Caleb like bullets, but he did his best to answer each one. "The staff said she caught the cross-town bus. I have no idea where she's headed. She could have gotten off anywhere north of here or transferred in another direction." He turned to LaGrange. "From the condition of the envelope, I don't think there was anything inside but paper." LaGrange inspected the envelope that had been left on the rolling table by the bed. "What do you expect to find?"

"This whole thing has been wonky from the beginning," LaGrange murmured.

"What's bothering you?" Ted asked.

"It's the kids," LaGrange answered. "We haven't had a single sighting, no calls for ransom, no one has offered a P.O.L. I've had men on Petrov since they disappeared, but they haven't seen a trace of either girl."

"What's a P.O.L.?" Caleb asked.

LaGrange hesitated, running his hands through his hair, but Ted answered for him. "Proof of life."

Caleb dropped into a chair. He hadn't considered the idea that the girls could be dead. This couldn't happen again. He couldn't survive losing another child, not to mention what it would do to Leah and Rosie.

"Think, Cal." Connor shook his shoulder. "Did Leah mention a place her dad took her to regularly? Maybe it's a park, or a library. Did she talk about wanting to take Belle someplace special?"

"Don't you think I've been wracking my brain ever since reading that letter? She never mentioned any special place." Caleb dropped his head into his hands. "I wish she'd answer her stupid phone. She turned off the ringer as soon as she got it so it wouldn't disturb Belle. I guess she never turned it back on. She's probably forgotten about it being in her purse."

"She has a phone with her?" LaGrange asked.

"That's it!" Ted exclaimed. "We can get those techy computer cops to track her phone like they do on TV."

"Can they do that?" Connor asked LaGrange.

"Well, yeah, but don't get excited. We'd have to get a warrant. That'll be tricky. Leah isn't considered a missing person yet. You can't just hack into someone's phone without their permission. It violates their privacy."

"I'll give you my consent." Caleb slowly stood. "That phone belongs to me. If necessary, I'll swear it was stolen."

****

Before beginning their twenty-minute journey east, through heavy Tampa traffic, Ivan took Leah's purse and threw it into the front passenger floorboard. A glass partition rose with a hum between them and the back door locks snapped. The knobs to unlock them were missing. She wouldn't be able to get out of the car until he released her. Obviously, any further conversation was impossible. She was trapped in the stench that seemed to be getting worse.

She knew the Tampa area as well as the freckles on her nose, and kept busy mentally noting every street sign and landmark. They were at the edge of town when the car slowed to a stop outside a narrow parking garage. The building attached to it had been a medical building, which had closed a few years earlier.

Ivan got out to move an orange construction barrier, and then replaced it once he moved the car inside. There was no electricity in the structure. Leah had never realized how badly overhead fluorescents were needed during the day. A gray glow from one open side was the only light to guide them to the third level that was, thankfully, an open rooftop.

Ivan parked to one side near a space taken by an ancient, four-door Impala. The other car was painted metallic purple and sat on tiny tires that caused its undercarriage to almost touch the ground. A young black male slid out of the driver's seat. Petrov awkwardly rolled out of the back, brushing white fake fur hairs off his pant legs from the upholstery. A look of irritation quickly turned to a smile when he saw Leah waiting to be let out of his trap.

"So glad you could join us, Ms. Fletcher." Petrov opened her door, and then stumbled away when the odor from the car reached him. He pressed the back of his index finger to his nostrils. "Oh my, we'll have to do something about that."

Leah inhaled the first deep breath she'd taken in half an hour. How long would it be before she could enjoy a long shower and have her clothes burned? She followed Petrov to the front of the other car. As she passed she noticed there was no one else inside. No car seat held her precious baby.

"Where are the children?" she cried. "You promised to return the children if I came here."

"I made no such promise." Petrov shrugged. "I

simply told you what could happen to children in my country. I'm sure I didn't mention anyone by name."

"Where are you hiding Yvonne and Belle? I know you're the one who has taken them."

"You took Yvonne Washington?" the younger man shouted. "It serves the little bitch right for helping her murdering mother and smearing Easy-T's rep."

Leah took a closer look at him "You're one of the men from the courthouse. You and your friend were in the hospital when the girls disappeared." She swung her head to face Petrov. "Now I know you're lying. You had them kidnapped."

"Sadly, no, it wasn't me." Petrov pouted. "However, I've always been good at taking advantage of an opportunity."

"The name's Killa-K, bitch." The young man straightened and puffed out his chest. "You'll find out why if you disrespect me, like Yvonne did Easy. If I'd taken that little rat-bitch, she'd be sent home in pieces by now."

Leah ignored Killa's outburst. "I came here to get mine and Rosie's daughters back."

"No," Petrov replied. "You came to pay what you owe me. I know you removed items from my house that contained the money your father stole."

"There was no money in those old trunks, just dolls and a clown costume my mother stored after my dad's death. If she found any money, I would have known."

"I don't believe Peggy found the money. If she had she would have died of an overdose the same day." Petrov removed a phone from his front pocket and typed a text message. "If you don't have my money, I guess you'll have to pay your father's debt another way."

"What are you talking about?" Before the words left Leah's mouth a black Lincoln Navigator rumbled up the entrance ramp. A muscle-bound, bald man descended from the driver's door. He placed a cap on his head that matched the one Ivan wore. His black suit was also similar. A pair of Oakley sunglasses hid his eyes. How had he made his way through the dimly lit levels of the garage wearing dark glasses? It didn't matter. Nothing mattered except getting the children back.

The new driver lifted the wide door at the back of the SUV and removed a metal and canvas contraption that folded out to make the largest and most elaborate chair this side of Buckingham Palace. A moment later, a small, gray haired man from the backseat made himself at home in the big chair.

"Ms. Fletcher, I'd like to introduce you to Eduard Pushkin. He leads an organization as well as an entertainment establishment, both called L'vov Logovo. In English that means Lion's Lair. I owe Mr. Pushkin an entertainer for his club and you owe me money. Isn't it wonderful that we've all come together?"

"I don't owe you anything and I'm not going anywhere." Leah turned to walk away, but Killa grabbed her arm.

"Mr. Petrov wants you to stay, bitch."

"You really need to expand your vocabulary, kid." Leah struck him under the nose with the heel of her hand. When he grabbed the bloody appendage with both hands, she drew her leg high and kicked him in the stomach. He fell to the ground like a puppet with its strings cut. Over his moan, she heard a metallic click and turned to face the barrel of Ivan's gun.

"Do try to be careful with my merchandise," Eduard requested. "She's no use to me dead and my clients won't be happy if she has disfiguring scars."

Chapter Thirty-Four

Petrov's amusement died when a familiar, clicking high-heel gait echoed in the cement structure. The sound came progressively closer. It couldn't be who he thought, but it was. In the next minute his dear cousin stood in the entry wearing tall leather boots with a tight, short dress under a long, lightweight coat, all in black. The outfit reminded him of the heroine of a movie he'd seen on television.

Something was different about her. She'd turned into a hard woman after the L'vov Logovo had owned her, but never with him. She'd sought his affection and approval. Now her stance was rigid and her eyes were empty as she glared at him. Perhaps she was in shock.

"Katya, my little kitten, where have you been? Why haven't you contacted me? I've been frantic since finding Adrik."

"How sweet, Bogdan," she cooed. "Were you afraid I wouldn't be protected? Have you forgotten how resourceful I can be? There was no need to worry. I have all the help I need." Katya snapped her fingers; two men came in behind her on soft-soled shoes. George had his long barrel, .45 Magnum pointed at Petrov. Carl aimed a 9-mm automatic at Pushkin.

"I didn't think you'd mind me taking over your employees now that you've succeeded in replacing them." Katya looked down at Killa-K, still curled on the floor after Leah's attack. An amused smirk curled her lips. "I suggest you all put your weapons on the ground and slide them my way."

Ivan and Pushkin's man dropped their guns and kicked them toward her. They couldn't risk the lives of their bosses. Both wore fierce expressions as Katya picked them up. "You too, little sewer rat," she told Killa.

He fumbled his .38 special from his waistband and threw it halfway to her.

"I'm surprised you'd trust the men who punished you in such a humiliating manner, my love." Petrov had to make her understand he was still her champion. She was too dangerous not to be on his side.

"They've paid for what you allowed them to do to me. Now, my revenge on you will be complete."

"But Katya, we've always been so close. No one has ever known me as well as you."

"That's right, cousin." She gave him a wicked smile. "I know everything. I know where the bodies are buried, where the keys are hidden, and which music box is your favorite."

"You!" Petrov bellowed. "You were in my house. You left evidence for the police to suspect me. I've nearly been driven crazy by your pranks. Why would you do such things to me?"

"Because of her." Katya pointed Ivan's small silver handgun at Leah. "All you cared about was the money her father took. I begged you to leave here, to go away with me, but she was more important. Her and that stupid money. I could have given you so much more. Instead, you sold me back to my tormentors." Katya thumbed the hammer back on the gun. "I'll see to it that she never gets in my way again."

Killa scrambled behind his purple Impala and crawled in the passenger door. He managed to squirm across to the driver's seat and turn the screwdriver handle protruding from the ignition. The car roared to life. "I didn't sign up for no shit like this!"

The car leaped forward. It struck the back of the Mercedes, causing its trunk lid to pop open. Killa's scream rang over the sound of the rumbling engine when he saw the bloated, bloody body of his best friend, Tug.

With an annoyed expression, Katya turned the gun and shot Killa behind his left ear.

"For heaven's sake, Bogdan," Pushkin groused. "Couldn't you have taken care of that mess before you came?"

****

Caleb was pressed against the wall of the exit ramp only a few feet from the opening to the rooftop level when his cell phone vibrated. It came from an unknown number, but he didn't worry, knowing he was so close to the children now.

His heart was still pounding from his trek through the dark garage. This was his hell, but if walking through hell saved Leah he'd do it gladly. That didn't mean Connor felt the same. How much could he ask his brother to endure given his past experience? Was it just his imagination or did the place actually smell like death?

Connor and Ted were waiting at the other end of the structure in the entrance ramp where they'd followed Katya and her two men. Had they seen the three latecomers take all the weapons and shoot the young gang member? Did they get a look at the body in the trunk? Were they aware of the gun aimed at Leah? They were all armed, but he prayed they wouldn't act in haste and get her killed. They needed a distraction to draw the woman's attention from Leah.

LaGrange came close and whispered, "I have units on the street and at the openings of each level. They've been instructed to stand down and stay quiet until we ensure your wife's safety."

Caleb knew it was only a slip of the tongue, but the word *wife* sent a shot of electricity through his system. He'd never thought of changing his relationship with Leah. They seemed comfortable the way it was. But, could he risk losing her to another man one day? She'd never indicated she wanted a commitment between them. She'd never asked for anything. Maybe she didn't think he'd come through for her any better than anyone else had. It was an avenue he'd have to explore, once they were back at home with Belle. The cops wanted him to stand down. Bullshit.

"I want my baby." Leah's demand was directed toward Katya.

"I don't have your brat." She grinned as she moved closer. "But, if I did, she'd be in a shallow grave by now."

Leah screamed and lunged. She grabbed the wrist that held the gun and shoved it aside. A stray bullet exploded. It struck Petrov's shoulder. Ivan ran to assist him.

It was the distraction Caleb needed. Suddenly police in heavy vests and carrying riot guns were running past them.

"Drop your weapons and put your hands behind

your heads!" LaGrange shouted.

Eduard Pushkin and his driver dove into their car. The engine roared to life. A cop's bullet ricocheted off the windshield.

Carl threw his hands in the air. "I know everything. I'll testify. Don't shoot."

George's shot struck the center of Carl's forehead before Connor could tackle him to the ground.

Katya crouched behind Pushkin's running car. The Russian boss lowered his window and shouted to her. "You have two choices, my dear, an American prison or L'vov Logovo."

Katya ran to the lip of the rooftop and jumped to the concrete sidewalk below.

Caleb didn't care about her or anyone but the woman in his arms. He stroked Leah's back as she sobbed. "My baby's gone Caleb. How am I ever going to find her?"

"I swear to you, Leah, I'll find her if it costs me my last breath. She's my baby too, and I love you both. We'll be a family. I'm going to bring her home and never let either of you out of my sight again." *God, help me.*

Caleb's phone vibrated again. Could this be the answer to his prayer? A message had been left from the unknown number he'd ignored a few minutes before. *Hello, Mr. McCrae. You don't know me, but I have Yvonne and your baby. Please call me back as soon as possible.*

It was the call he'd been waiting for. He prayed one more time. *Please, God, let them be all right and bring them home to us.* Caleb punched the callback button and waited as the phone rang three times.

"Hello?"

"This is Caleb McCrae. Are the children safe?"

"Mr. McCrae, I can't tell you how sorry I am for your worry. My name is Dorothia Bishop. Yvonne and my girl, Brooklyn, have been friends since first grade. I came home from my shift at the glass plant this morning and found her and your baby hiding in Brooklyn's room. It took half the day to get her to tell me where that sweet little child belongs."

"Did she tell you why she took the baby?" Caleb asked.

"She says a couple of hoodlums from the old neighborhood were watching your wife at the hospital. She got scared and ran. I know them boys, Mr. McCrae. They are bad news."

"You won't have to worry about them any more." Caleb reluctantly glanced toward the body in the trunk of Petrov's car.

"I guess Yvonne figured this would be a good place to hide because she knew we always keep plenty of diapers and baby formula for the grandkids when they visit. She really is a good girl, Mr. McCrae. I couldn't call the police on her. I know she was just trying to protect little Belle. I hope you won't be too hard on her."

"That'll be up to her mother. All I want is to bring them home. I'll be glad to reimburse you for any supplies."

Chapter Thirty-Five

Caleb's chest swelled with pride every time the sunlight sparkled against the diamond on Leah's finger. It didn't matter that she wore shorts and an old T-shirt while she packed. She hadn't taken it off since she'd accepted it two months earlier. At her insistence, they planned to marry in their own backyard, as soon as they settled in to their new house.

It had been hard for Peggy to accept that her childhood home had been leveled to make way for a neighborhood playground, but she had a nice apartment in an assisted living facility for recovering addicts. She was looking forward to a fresh start with her daughter and granddaughter, but that would require taking baby steps for all of them.

It had been easy for him to help her obtain a divorce once she'd filed assault charges against Bogdan Petrov. The Russian admitted throwing his wife down the stairs. It was the least of his worries when faced with multiple murder charges that would keep him in prison for the rest of his life. There was nothing his lawyer could do in light of the deal the prosecutor's office had made with Ivan. However, the crooked counselor didn't hesitate to confiscate Petrov's collection of antique music boxes to cover his fee.

Miss Hannah's plans had been held up for a little while, but she'd soon return with Connor's family for the wedding, and resume her regular duties. Clarice would then be free to move south and begin her new job in Connor's Mayville office. She made Rosie promise to finish her business courses and give Yvonne a better life. Caleb was determined to help her keep that promise by providing free room and board for as long as necessary.

When Belle woke with a hearty wail, he followed a trail between the boxes and trunks to her crib. She'd recently found her fingers and toes, and was just as happy and secure in her daddy's arms as she was with her mom. Thankfully, she was oblivious to all they'd been through during her disappearance. He had Yvonne to thank for that. The young teen had used what resources she knew to keep his baby safe when Tug and Killa-K followed Leah in the hospital cafeteria.

Caleb still thought about his first child, Angel, all the time. He decided that everything had worked out the way it had because Belle's big sister was looking out for her. He took comfort in the thought that she always would.

"Mr. Caleb." Yvonne held up a red-nosed doll, almost her size. "I don't think this clown is a fit toy for little Belle's new nursery."

"But, it's my favorite," Leah remarked. "It was the last one my father gave me."

"It has sharp parts." Yvonne showed them a bead of blood on her index finger. "It's not safe."

"Let me see that thing." Rosie abandoned her packing to inspect the doll. "It has metal staples in the back seam."

"I don't remember that." Leah took the doll and manipulated the staples loose.

"Here's another one." Rosie worked on a slightly smaller clown.

"This one too," Yvonne called.

In minutes, all their laps were covered in bundles of money.

"This must be Petrov's money," Leah exclaimed. "What do we do with it?"

"It never belonged to Petrov," Caleb said. "Your dad stole it from a man who refused to report it missing. He'd probably come into it illegally. He died a few years later, leaving his estate to charity. Technically, it doesn't belong to anyone."

"I'll take it!" Marcus had walked into the room.

All the money was stacked and counted. It was the exact amount Petrov had claimed. Caleb opened a safe in his closet to store it until he could talk to his father and brother. When he returned to the sitting room, Marcus was surrounded by the women as he played with the baby.

"Did I forget that Belle had a checkup scheduled?"

"Umm, no…"

"Marcus came by to give me a ride," Rosie said. "He's taking me to a restaurant, and then maybe a movie."

****

One year later:

Caleb stood by as Peggy tied a balloon to the front of Belle's stroller. The baby squealed with delight. Hot dogs, cotton candy, and a live band gave the event a carnival atmosphere. A large sign by the road announced the grand opening of the *New Beginnings Birthing Center*.

"The place is spectacular," Dr. Falstaff declared.

"You've provided state of the art equipment, a relaxed and comfortable atmosphere, top of the line electronics. I'm beyond pleased to sponsor such a great clinic. It's just what the community needed."

"Marcus should get the credit," Caleb admitted. "He worked his butt off to get his midwifery license. He handpicked each member of the staff, you know. After the way he took care of Leah and Belle, it was a pleasure to make his dream a reality. Besides that, Leah funded the whole thing. After investing the money, it grew like wild fire. Then, she pestered everyone in town to donate what they could. Not many businesses can brag to opening without a black cloud in the form of a loan over its head."

"Where is your lovely wife?"

"She went inside with Marcus and Rosie," Peggy said. "They had some paperwork to take care of."

"They should be out here enjoying the fun," Dr. Falstaff said. "This is no time to be working."

Caleb wheeled his daughter into Rosie's office. She'd put the nameplate he had made for her on the front edge of her new desk. Leah sat in a chair at the side while Rosie clicked away at her computer. Marcus watched his office manager with admiration. Was that also a glimmer of affection in his eyes? A romance between the two had been brewing since they met.

"You're all missing the party."

"We'll only be a few minutes," Leah told him.

"What's more important than this grand opening?" he asked. The women looked at each other and Leah gave Rosie a nod.

"I'm signing up our first patient," Rosie said.

A word from the author...

From childhood I've moved from place to place, from Indiana to Florida, stopping in several places in between. I also moved from job to job: as a waitress, soldier, retail manager, dental assistant, etc. The one thing I never had to leave behind was my imagination.

Storytelling has always been my favorite way to pass time. I've often been told I should write a book. Finally, I did. It was so much fun; I feel I must write more.

I've been a student of Long Ridge Writers Group and once won a short story contest with Harlequin.

I currently live in north Florida with my husband, whom I torture with crazy story lines and half-written manuscripts. He has put up with me for thirty-plus years.

Thank you for purchasing
this publication of The Wild Rose Press, Inc.

If you enjoyed the story, we would appreciate your
letting others know by leaving a review.

For other wonderful stories,
please visit our on-line bookstore at
www.thewildrosepress.com.

For questions or more information
contact us at
info@thewildrosepress.com.

The Wild Rose Press, Inc.
www.thewildrosepress.com

Stay current with The Wild Rose Press, Inc.

Like us on Facebook

https://www.facebook.com/TheWildRosePress

And Follow us on Twitter
https://twitter.com/WildRosePress